FLAGS OUT FRONT

FLAGS OUT FRONT

A CONTRARIAN'S DAYDREAM

》》X《《

Douglas Wilson

canonpress
Moscow, Idaho

Published by Canon Press
P.O. Box 8729, Moscow, Idaho 83843
800.488.2034 | www.canonpress.com

Douglas Wilson, *Flags Out Front: A Contrarian's Daydream*
Copyright ©2017 by Douglas Wilson.

Interior layout by Valerie Anne Bost.
Cover design by James Engerbretson.
Cover illustration by Forrest Dickison.

Printed in the United States of America.

Library of Congress Cataloging-in-Publication Data is forthcoming.

17 18 19 20 21 22 23 24   10 9 8 7 6 5 4 3 2 1

For George and Karen Grant,
with many thanks.

CONTENTS

I. FREEDOM OF EXPRESSION

CHOCTAW VALLEY BIBLE COLLEGE WAS NESTLED (as I believe the expression goes) on fifty acres at the head of the valley whose name it shared—Choctaw Valley, that is, not Bible College Valley. There were no paved roads that made their way through the hills up behind the school, and so, for those motorists who took it into their heads to drive up the valley on Sunday afternoons, the college grounds served as a steeply sloped and very green dead end. In the autumn it was a very golden-red dead end, but the driving realities were not altered by any of that.

The small school was a dead end in other ways also, but a significant gift from a wealthy alumnus, generous after the fashion of old cotton, had helped to mask that reality from most outside observers. One person from whom that reality was *not* masked was the president, a likable but evidently mild man named Tom Collins. He came from teetotaling stock, and so it should be noted he was named after a favorite uncle, and not after the cocktail.

Despite being lean and muscular, at least for a forty-five-year-old, Tom had a good-natured mildness that was universally recognized by all, for it was the only attribute that had ever had occasion to be presented to the outside world. But President Collins had himself some hidden reserves, an aquifer of moxie far beneath the deepest wells he had ever had to use. But even *he* didn't know about any of that, and I am running ahead. All the writers' workshops say not to do that, and especially not in the third paragraph.

Tom Collins, known and beloved by the students as Dr. Tom, knew that the college was drifting slowly downward—not so much mission drift as plain old gravity drift—and he had known this since before he had first taken on the job five years before. He also knew that the endowment wasn't fixing anything *really*, new dorms or no new dorms, and that something else was going to have to do the fixing, if any fixing were to happen. Though he had no idea what that might be, he did think and pray about it quite a bit.

It was a September morning, very early, and an afterglow-drunk sophomore from a community college at the mouth of the valley was driving home for a few hours in the sack before he failed to get up for his first class. As it happened, he was driving right past the Bible college, just as he always did in order to get back home again. But as the hour was very early, and there was no one in sight in any direction, the student's eye was suddenly arrested by the three flagpoles just inside the entry drive of the college. The student was named Marc . . . not that it really matters . . . but his name was Marc. Pretty sure it was Marc. The central flag pole carried the American flag, and the two shorter ones on either side were for the Christian flag and the state flag, respectively. Marc pulled over by the side of the road and stared malevolently. "Jesus and the two thieves," he muttered, and got out of the car.

After a few moments of quick work, the flags were all rearranged, as he would have put it (in fact as he *did* put it to himself in the car afterward), just for the hell of it. But he was still technically drunk and couldn't be expected to know not to use that kind of language on the grounds of a Bible college. The Christian flag was now flying high above the others, the state flag was where the Christian flag had been, and the American flag was where the state flag had been. Marc got back into the car, hugely pleased with himself, and headed home to bed, and clean right out of the story. But there were ripples, as they say, in his wake.

Dr. Tom came into work very early that same day, and so he arrived about forty-five minutes after the great flag switch. He turned into the entryway, flanked on both sides with a sweeping red brick wall, curved like welcoming arms, the left side emblazoned with *Choctaw Valley* and the right side with *Bible College*. Something was funny, not right. He slowed the car down to try to get a better sense of it. He glanced up through the windshield again, started violently, slammed on the brakes, and then jumped out of the car. He stood looking at the flags for a good five minutes, stupefied.

Since his wife Darla had passed away six years before, he had noticed that he had been more emotional than he had ever been before, so maybe that was it. Close to the surface, that kind of thing. So, in passing, he felt that his eyes were kind of weepy, but it was not anything that anybody else would have noticed if they had been there. But the predominant thing, the thing that took up all the oxygen in his internal room, was an indescribable thrill, the kind of thing that he had only felt once before in his life—back when he was twelve, when he had dedicated himself to ministry at that revival over in Parkersville. He hadn't thought about *that* in years, come to think of it, but he felt exactly the same way now, and had no earthly idea why. When he saw the flags that way, the thrill had swept over the top of him and settled back down in the bottoms of his shoes. He stood another minute more, then quietly got back into his car, and drove slowly up the drive.

As he drove, the words he had memorized as a boy through the course of numerous opening ceremonies, the ones starting each day of Vacation Bible School, came back to him. *I pledge allegiance to the Christian Flag and to the Savior for whose Kingdom it stands. One Savior, crucified, risen, and coming again with life and liberty to all who believe.* Well, if that is what the flag means, then a *Bible* college, of all things, had no business flying it in any kind of second-fiddle position.

>>>X<<<

The first call came at 9:34 a.m., from a Mrs. McCorkadale— the chairman, as she identified herself, of a local civic women's group. She was quite pleasant and businesslike at the beginning. "I was calling to inquire," she said, "if you were aware of the *insult* to the American flag that is taking place just inside the gates of your college."

"I am aware of no insult," he said. "It must be some kind of misunderstanding..."

"Someone has removed the American flag from its proper place, and it is now occupying one of the lesser flagpoles."

"Oh, that," he said. "Yes, I did see that coming in this morning. Is that what you meant?"

"You *saw* that? And you did nothing? This is intolerable, outrageous. I insist that the flag be restored to its rightful place of honor immediately!"

Well, this was it. Here we were. Caesar had his Rubicon. What did Bible college presidents have? A Rubik's Cube? All his instincts were in favor of mollification. He naturally turned his mind to ways that he could reassure Mrs. McCorkadale. She was a nice woman. Meant well. Civic minded. In short, his instincts were clamoring for some sort of rapprochement. But he had decided. He thought of that revival back at Parkersville. Dr. Tom took a deep breath, held it for a moment, exhaled silently, and then said, "No. No, I think we will leave it this way."

The click on the other end of the line was a lot louder than it usually is. *Mrs. McCorkadale.* Where had he heard that name before? He was pretty sure he had met her. He pulled open one of his desk drawers, pulled out a community directory, and started flipping through it. He had only gotten to the D's when he stopped and whistled. The group that Mrs. McCorkadale was chairman of was Daughters of the Confederacy. Tom Collins rubbed his chin, and wondered what was coming next. The early returns were promising—this was going to be one of life's chapters that is full of pleasant and edifying instruction.

>>><<<

The eruption that followed was gorgeous and overdone, and was actually due to a couple of factors. One of them was that there was virtually nothing going on anywhere in the world. Say you were in a cafeteria with five hundred people in it, just as maybe you have been once, eating and chattering and clattering and everything, and then suddenly, for no reason, everybody went quiet at the same time, except for you. It was like that. The number of compelling human interest stories had plummeted, and the number of twenty-four-hour cable news channels had not plummeted. No news, no interesting wars, and no celebrity meltdowns were to be had anywhere. Slow news days dragged a couple of slow news weeks after them like a wet rope, and producers of news programs were starting to get desperate.

The other big factor was that there had been an infamous flag desecration case at what Dr. Tom called Behemoth State, that famous land of knowledge, just the previous year, and the university in question was only an hour or so away from Choctaw Valley. The decision that came down from the federal circuit court had favored the defendant, a long-haired hippie from another part of the country *entirely*, a place where it snowed on Yankees, a fellow who, in the course of a strident protest over something important, had peed on the flag on the front steps of the administration building. Feelings over *that* were still raw throughout the entire region. The decision favoring the defendant was written by a Carter appointee, a gentleman who had peed on the flag himself back in the glory days of the sixties, and who therefore did himself proud as he wrote up the decision. Thinking himself most courageous, he

had written expansively and in sweeping terms, and had un-
wittingly left a hole large enough for a drunken community
college sophomore named Marc to stumble through. (Pretty
sure it was Marc.) "There is *nothing* that can be done with
or to our precious flag," the judge had written, "that should
ever cause us to flinch or step back from our commitment to
absolute freedom of expression, which is, after all, what this
precious flag represents."

The italics were in the *original*, and by the time the whole
Dr. Tom thing was over, attorneys for various groups were
bent entirely out of their original shape and didn't know what
to do with themselves anymore. One ACLU attorney named
Greenbaum was particularly flummoxed, and spoke quite
sharply to his colleagues about it. "Urination I understand,
and defecation I understand. Setting the damn thing on fire
is clearly protected speech. That's why we come to work in the
morning. That's why we're here. That's what freedom means.
But subordinated *honor*? That is just creepy."

〉〉〉X〈〈〈

The development officer for Choctaw Valley was usually
all grins and spectacles, always ready with a hearty hand-
shake. He was the man who had masterminded the cotton
legacy endowment. He was invaluable to the college, and the
college knew it right well. He knew that the college knew it,

and his name was Don Carpenter. "Donnie" to those who gave in the six-figure range.

Don Carpenter was now walking thoughtfully toward Dr. Tom's office, head bowed under the weight of the weighty thoughts he was going to have to bring in with him. They were so weighty he had to carry them around in an invisible duffel bag. President Collins smiled when he saw him, and gestured expansively to the two wingbacks off to the side of his desk. He liked Don, despite his slightly overdone professionalism.

"Good to see you, Don," Tom said. "What's on development's plate this week?" They usually met on Friday, and this was Wednesday, and Tom was surprised he hadn't gotten this visit already. But Don . . . he knew Don . . . probably wanted to position himself like he was really open, could really go either way, had thought it through, which meant that he couldn't really be in Tom's office applying the pressures of donors and their realities half an hour after the controversy had made the news. Give it a couple of hours at least. Don was a master of timing. After all, as a sage once put it, the only difference between salad and garbage is timing.

Don scratched his chin thoughtfully, as he always did without thinking whenever he was going to say something he thought would be heard with something less than gladness by his auditor. "Well, Tom, it's like this . . . I haven't actually had to answer any calls on this flag business as of yet, but I can safely anticipate that I will have to pretty soon. And . . . just wanted to check . . . do you feel you have really thought this thing through? Taken counsel, that kind of thing?"

"Well, I haven't really thought it through—there hasn't been time really. It is not as though this were part of some kind of plan . . . it just happened."

"Exactly," Don said. "My concern exactly. If we haven't really thought it through, and it could have repercussions to our donor base—not saying it will, but it probably will—then ought we not take it slowly? Go back to the *status quo ante*, ask a committee of the faculty to have a look see, and play it safe? Future of the college at stake, Tom." Don's right eyebrow was arched with deep concern.

"Know what you're saying, Don. But hand to the plow and all that."

"Okay, you're the boss. Just wanted you to know the almost certain costs involved. Something in the Bible about that too, you know. Nobody wants a half-finished tower." Don opened the door slowly, and shook his head with grave wisdom as it slowly closed behind him, and he took his duffel bag full of sorrows down the hallway with him.

>>>X<<<

Later that afternoon, Maria came in, looked over her shoulder, and closed the door behind her. She had been the administrative assistant for the previous president, and as she was extremely competent, it had been the easiest thing in the world for Dr. Tom to keep her on. Why wouldn't he keep her on?

"May I speak to you for a moment?" she said. "I mean, not in the course of my official duties? I don't want to intrude myself . . ."

"Certainly, certainly," Tom said. He was sitting behind his desk, with a legal pad on his knees. He got up and came around the desk.

"Well, there are two things," she said. "I was talking to my father about all this," and with *all this* she gestured expansively in a way that encompassed the rearranged flags out in front. "And when he was in the Navy, he said that whenever divine services were in session on a ship of the line, the Christian flag was raised higher than the American flag. I don't know if they do that *still*, but I thought it was really interesting. You might want to have the attorney . . . ?" She trailed off.

Tom nodded. "Good. That's very good. We can use anything like that. Even as a historical precedent, that's good." Tom scribbled a few notes on the pad he was holding.

"The second thing is . . . is . . ." Maria looked over her shoulder at the closed door again. Then she looked at the floor. "I . . . I wanted to tell you that I am *very* proud to be working here." And with that, she stepped forward impulsively, kissed him on the cheek, stepped back with eyes wide open. She then retreated through the door and back to her desk abashed, hurling silent insults at herself as she went. It was not until she was back at her desk that she realized, with a mixture of relief and sadness and some more relief again, that she had not kissed him on the cheek at all. That was only a real-time daydream, in slow-mo. But she *had* said that she was proud to be working there. And she was too.

But as the door closed behind her, Tom touched his cheek cautiously, and then wondered why he had done that. "Huh," he thought.

)))X(((

Don came through the door two days later, chortling and grinning. "Five hundred eighty-two requests for admission applications. I'm thinking there might be something to this thing of yours. We have never seen anything like this before. I would urge you, in the strongest possible terms, to stick to your principles. Never compromise on principle. One of the things that made this college the pride of Choctaw Valley." Then he held up his hand. "I know, I know . . ."

President Tom raised his coffee mug and grinned into it. "Any other news from your department?"

"Well, yes," Don reached into his stack and pulled out another manila folder from his stack, "now that you mention it. I have received about thirteen calls . . ." he counted silently, " Yes, thirteen calls from donors from previous years who had all begged off some time ago. They had given some of the standard, generic reasons at the time—restructuring priorities and all that code talk. But over half of these folks who called back told me that they had actually discontinued giving because they thought the college was going soft, or liberal, or neo-evangelical, or something. Giving is up thirty percent from this time last year. Last month we were dragging at about five percent behind."

"And what do we take away from all this?" Tom asked.

"Like I said. Principles are the thing. Without that, we might as well be a state school for electronics repair. Obviously, you can't ever do this kind of thing for calculated reasons—pragmatic manipulation of principle isn't principled—but it has often occurred to me that it would be nice for us if we could. I think I mentioned something about that last time we talked."

Tom grinned again, and Don held his hand up again.

>>><<<

The chairman of the college's board of trustees was named Peter Kramer, and he was a gruff specimen. Tom had once, years before, described him to Darla as one tough baby. He was an honest man of principle, and Tom had differed with him more than with all the other trustees put together. And so when Peter Kramer appeared in the doorway one afternoon, Tom thought to himself, understandably, that the ax was about to fall. *It was a nice job*, he thought. *Perhaps it was not too late to figure out a solution. Perhaps he could keep his job.* Dr. Tom could feel his mind rummaging in the basement of his conscience, looking for a way out. None had been found, but a lot of boxes had been emptied out.

"You know, Tom," Kramer said, settling in his chair, "I have served together on this board for fifteen years with you, the last six of that with you here as president, and this is the first time it has ever occurred to me that you might have a real spine."

Tom smiled widely at that, and Peter Kramer held up his hand. "No, no, don't take that wrong. Sorry. That came out pretty bad. It's not that I ever thought you were spineless, like a coward or anything. It is just that the question never presented itself, and, if it had, I most certainly would have guessed that you would have come down on the amicable and peaceable side of things. I always took you for a lover, not a fighter. You have really surprised me, is all."

"Well," Dr. Tom said. "I have to say that I am kind of surprised myself. Truth be told."

"How are you doing?" Kramer said, not unkindly.

"Well, since I just used that phrase 'truth be told,' I should probably also tell you that I alternate between states of buzzed exhilaration and high panic. If that happens more than three times, it can make for an interesting half hour."

"So may I tell you why I am here?" Kramer asked.

Sure thing, Tom nodded.

"I have spent a big chunk of yesterday going over our by-laws, policy manual, the accreditation report we just got last spring, and your contract with us. I read all the way through *Robert's Rules of Order,* which I have been meaning to do any-way. A lot of interesting stuff in there, by the way, believe it or not. I am the chair of the board for the next two years, and that means that you don't need to worry about any internal coup. You are as safe as it gets on that front, at least as far as it depends on me. Don't go wobbly on me, boyo, and it doesn't matter how much some of the other trustees fret, fulminate, or send emails, you have two years in which to weather this thing. And I know at least a couple of trustees have been as impressed as I was. As long as you don't show up in some newspaper pho-to with a couple of New Orleans hookers in tow, your job is safe for the time being. Don't go wobbly, and we have your back. Don't give way to fear. Dogs can smell fear."

"Dogs?"

"A metaphor. Got away from me. Don't go wobbly, I like that word, and things are fine. Our fine governor is running for president, and he's got that *look* in his eye, so we can't keep you out of jail or anything. But if you wind up there, you will be there as the president of Choctaw Valley Bible College."

"Thanks much," Dr. Tom said. "You enjoying this?"

"Yes, frankly," Kramer said. "You?"

Tom grinned. "Not yet. But I have been thinking about it."

2. THE BATTLE OF CHOCTAW VALLEY

THE MAIN DRIVE OF THE COLLEGE RAN STRAIGHT north from the gate before being rudely interrupted by a little circle that wrapped adroitly around the aforementioned small mound where the three flag poles were standing tall. It then continued, free of that brief entanglement, in a straight shot up to the administration building. On the second floor of that admin building, directly above the central doors, was a wide set of windows that was accustomed to usher the bright daylight into Tom's office every morning. He was standing at that set of windows now, gazing out past the front gate at the milling people, scores of them.

As it happened, a satellite television truck was parked right where that drunk kid Marc had parked when he first perpetrated the great flag misdeed. Another one was parked right where Tom had stopped his car to look at the great flag misdeed. And by merely looking at the flag misdeed, and deciding to do nothing about it, Dr. Tom had elevated a drunken prank into a national crisis. Oh, well. All around those two trucks was a rapidly assembling crowd. Dr. Tom could see people streaming up the road from the stadium parking lot.

The rally "for the flag" was set for ten a.m.—late enough to get a good crowd, and not so late that the expected September heat would cook them out of there. The citizenry had started to come in about half an hour beforehand, with most of the fauna identifiable as representative of the same tribe as the organizer of the rally—Mrs. Patricia McCorkadale. At the same time, there were specimens from the Left . . . over *on* the left, as it turns out. Those on the right were standing around confusedly, while those on the left were occupying confusedly. There were no community organizers with megaphones yet.

Having disparate elements from both left and right didn't just happen by accident. There had been a tentative invitation from Mrs. McCorkadale, some tense negotiations, some *whatabouts* offered by both sides, and an agreement between them to act the part of co-belligerents, at least for the day. One group wanted the American flag *up*, while the other wanted the Christian flag *down*, and it seemed to them that for a time that they could row to the same coxswain.

"But keep your people over on the left," Mrs. McCorkadale had said. They were wary of each other, but, speaking frankly, not nearly wary enough. (Even with that said, everything *would* have been fine for them all had they taken a young man named Trevor into account, but they hadn't. Trevor was a student at the college, there on a wildcard scholarship. Had the poet Burns been there, and had *he* met Trevor, he probably would have muttered something about what best-laid schemes tend to do, which is *gang aft agley*.)

There was a slight breeze that occasionally rustled the flags that were the point of contention, but which also kept the temperature down. The day was a beautiful one, and the birds in the surrounding foliage, unaware of the human drama that was gathering down below them on the asphalt, just continued on with their melodious ruckus.

The rally was located squarely in front of the main gate of the college, forcing all the cars of faculty and students to go in and out by the west gate. When the groundskeeper had first seen the crowd forming and the first few hand-made signs, he made a command decision, closed and locked the iron gates, and then called the president's office to give them a heads up.

An intern from the senior class, a very pretty brunette named Eve Halliday who worked with Maria, had taken the call and passed the information on to Maria, who went in to see Dr. Tom about it. As soon as she disappeared through the

door to his office, Eve whipped out her cell phone, and sent
a text to her roommate, a good sport named Tracy. "Tell the
guys that a protest rally on the flag thing is forming outside
the main gate. Wish we could mess with them." It was a de-
cisive wish. About thirty seconds later that *zzchhoop* sound
came back with a brief acknowledgment. "Kay."

Eve was a newcomer, a transfer student from Prairie Bible
Institute in Alberta. She had applied for the internship position on a last minute long shot, using the whole thing as a
fleece. If she got it, and there were multiple intelligent reasons
for thinking she couldn't and wouldn't, she would take that
as guidance. PBI and Choctaw Valley had a robust relationship when it came to the transfer of credits, which meant she
could finish out her senior year in the South and still take her
diploma from Prairie—something that both her mother and
grandmother had done. She had never been out of Alberta
before in her life, and in her weeks at Choctaw she had already seen more excitement than she had ever seen up on the
tundra. She had grown up a great deal north of Prairie, which
is saying something, and what her childhood surroundings
gave her in the way of big sky vistas, they had lacked in terms
of emotional drama.

Her father was an oil man, a man experienced in the ways
of getting oil up through that tundra, so he was one who
didn't really care about the lack of excitement. She loved
her family, and loved her home, but nonetheless . . . she was

highly pleased with this controversy that had erupted shortly after she had arrived. She was having some difficulty entering *fully* into the proceedings because none of the flags involved had a maple leaf on them, but she understood the principle of the thing and was doing all right.

About fifteen minutes later, as a result of Tracy's exertions in response to Eve's text, about thirty students met up in front of the library, which was right inside the west gate, and about fifty yards down the road from the main gate. Their leader, although never formally elected to be such, was the Trevor whom the poet Burns had never had the pleasure of meeting. He was a sturdy young man—a fellow that people usually considered good looking, eventually and somewhat reluctantly, after they had gotten over their first shock. Trevor was an acquired taste. But he had followed the flag controversy with great interest from the first day, and he was born ready to rumble.

On his way to the meeting by the library, Trevor had made it a point to walk across the lawn just inside the main gate in order to case the crowd that was forming.

"How many are there?" Miriam wanted to know. Miriam lived across the hall from Eve and Tracy.

"Looks like five hundred or so, and more coming up the road. And a couple satellite news trucks. I think they will get all the footage they need. Unless we disrupt it somehow . . ."

"What can we do? There are hardly any of us . . ."

Trevor had been reading in Samuel recently. "The Lord can save by few or by many, whether with or without an armor bearer."

"Right, but is the Lord going to do that with us having a plan or not? Or does having a plan constitute a lack of faith?"

Trevor tousled his hair with both hands. "A plan would be fine. What we need to do is this. There were some hippies over one on the west side, closest to us. You guys . . ." And here Trevor gestured to about five of them, all in the music leader program together. "You know how to sing, you know, projecting from the diaphragm and all of that stuff. You go get in the middle of that bunch, and start singing 'God Bless America.' You know the words?"

"'Stand beside her and guide her,' check." A junior named Caleb nodded his head.

"And then the rest of us will go deep into enemy territory, on the east side, where most of these people are, and see if we can shake something loose by doing something else. I'll have to think of that something on the way. But I think I have the general idea."

Sally, the chief of the musicians, nodded. "Don't we have to synchronize our watches or something?"

Kim shook her head. "No, we all have phones. Nobody has watches anymore. And the satellites synchronize them for us. Don't they?"

Trevor interrupted. "It doesn't matter, actually. We'll just key off you. Just let us get into position, and then start. But make sure we can hear you."

As they walked out the west gate, and down the road, the excitement soon swallowed up their nervousness. A number of people had parked further up the road, and were walking down toward the rally, and so the students blended in with the gathering crowd nicely. To the extent that anyone noticed students from the Bible school joining them, they thought it was nice that some of the kids were taking a stand for the flag too.

After they reached the main crowd, they wound their way through. The musicians stopped in the middle of the tie-dyed and dreadlocked group and waited for a few minutes so that Trevor's crew would have time to get in place. Then Sally looked around at her friends, nodded a little nervously, and blew a D on her pitch pipe. "God bless America . . ." They all started in. Everybody around them just turned and stared. "What are you doing?" one of them shouted. "The deal was that you would stay on your side," shouted another. "That was the *deal*!"

The students *did* know how to project, courtesy of Dr. Draper's unrelenting instruction on singing with your whole body, and in a minute some of the folks on the other side of the crowd, over on the right wing, started to pick it up as well. "To the oceans, white with foam . . ." And just as they were settling well into it, Trevor started clapping his hands rhythmically, but off tempo from "God Bless America." "Down with Jesus! Down with his flag! Down with Jesus! Down with his flag!" His fellow students joined in less enthusiastically.

A fellow in a tricorner hat stopped singing, and wheeled on Trevor, and the rest of the students with him who had taken up the chant. "What? *What* are they saying?"

"They's saying *down with Jesus*, Elmore." His wife had gone white in the face.

"Here, stop that," he said to Trevor. "We don't hold no truck with your down-with-Jesus socialism."

Trevor stopped and looked at him. "But that's His flag up there. And you want it down, don't you?"

"No, we want the American flag *up*."

"And Jesus' flag down, right?"

"Well . . ." Elmore stopped, and looked at his wife, baffled.

A more pugnacious-looking fellow than Elmore, who was on the other side of him, pulled on Elmore's sleeve, and said, "What're they saying?" A little cloth oval on his mechanic's uniform identified him as Bob.

Elmore looked around. "They're saying, 'Down with Jesus, down with His flag.'"

Bob didn't need any time to think over what *he* thought of this, being from childhood a man of action. He vaulted past Elmore in order to deliver a haymaker at the side of Trevor's head. But haymakers being what they are, Trevor saw it coming about fifteen minutes beforehand, and stepped adroitly aside. Bob connected solidly with one of Trevor's companions, Ken, knocking him sideways into some patriots on the other side of him. One of them did not take it kindly, and threw an elbow, connecting in a bone-grindy way with Bob's left eye socket. A melee promptly began, and matters were not helped by one of the television crews arriving immediately, and shoving their telephoto lenses into the fray. Trevor ducked down and slipped toward the back of the crowd, beckoning to the others to follow him. *This was living large.*

As these events were unfolding on the right side, the other news crew from the other satellite truck was busy filming a group of refugees from the Renaissance Fair yelling high obscenities at the "God Bless America" musician-theocrats. The discrepancy between the different kinds of footage the two crews got was striking, and led to no little consternation in the general public when their respective stories aired. The setup shots were exactly the same, mostly involving the grounds and flag poles of the college, but the stories were completely different. One had aging hippies cussing out clean-cut American youths, and the other had decent, hard-working, tax-paying Americans exchanging furious blows with one another. And both of them were doing this right smack in front of Choctaw Valley Bible College.

Trevor set up his remaining troops at a different place in the crowd and told them to do the same thing again: "Down with Jesus! Down with His flag!" They started in as before, and the results, while not resulting in fisticuffs like the first time, were chaotic in quite an adequate way. When that second round got going, Trevor pulled Tracy aside. "Do we have anybody who can call around and get us more reinforcements?"

Tracy nodded. "Eve could do that. She's my new room-mate. She's at work right now in Dr. Tom's office."

"Who could she call? And what's her cell number?"

Tracy looked at the time on her phone. "I couldn't get hold of Darren earlier, or Sue Nell, or Jim. They were all in class. They should be out now. Eve could get them—she has all their numbers." Tracy hurriedly gave him Eve's number. Trevor nodded, and Tracy went back to the agitators, who had moved on to a third location.

By this time, the entire front of the crowd on the right side was singing "God Bless America" and had begun to notice that their song leaders on the left were being cussed out. A certain restlessness began to set in.

Trevor trotted to the back of the mob, got free enough to be able to hear, and punched in the digits. The phone rang twice, and then a voice—"This is Eve."

This is Eve. Trevor had never heard anything so musical in his life, not even in the famous fourth quarter of Dr. Draper's appreciation course. The fumes of battle were wafting by him, every moment was critical, he was the informal gen-eral, and this musical voice had blown the three names that Tracy had given him clean out of his head. He was staggered. *What a voice.*

"This is Trevor," he finally managed. "Friend of Tracy's. Hold on a second." He gestured wildly at Tracy, who came scurrying over. "What were those names again?"

Tracy made a face at him. "Darren, Sue Nell, and Jim."

"Got it. Sorry." Trevor spoke into the phone again. "Eve, sorry about that. Could you call Darren, Sue Nell, and Jim? Tell them to get as many of us as they can round up in five minutes or they're going to miss out in a big way. Have them come out the west gate, and meet me at the back of the crowd. I'll be standing by the statue of Whitefield. Thanks so much."

Trevor hung up, and allowed himself a minute of reverie. *That voice! Why hadn't he heard that voice before? Why wasn't that voice sitting beside him, asking him what he wanted for dinner?*

》》X《《

Eve got right to her appointed task, and was successful with all three. Two of them were already with a large group, and were able to head to the west gate straight away. The third, Sue Nell, was about five minutes behind them, with about ten friends.

When she was done with her calls, she looked up, and saw that the door to Dr. Tom's office was open, and Maria was still in there. She got up, glanced in, and could see them both standing at the window, looking out across the admin lawn at the humanity frothing and tossing outside the main gate. She tapped on the door, and then tapped again. "Excuse me?"

"Come in," Dr. Tom said loudly.

Eve crossed the large office and came around the desk that was centered in front of the window. From where they stood, they could see some agitation stage right, and about three well-developed skirmishes on their left. There seemed to be two crowds. Two-thirds of the mob were on one side and one-third on the other, with the border between them surging uneasily. In the back, by the statue of Whitefield one person was standing. Every few minutes a cluster of people would come up to him, and he would direct them into different places in the crowd. In between the groups, he would climb up on the pedestal of the statue to get a better view of things.

"Does anybody know who that is?" Dr. Tom asked.

"His name is Trevor. I don't know anything more than that," Eve said.

"That must be Trevor Smith," Maria said. "We only have three Trevors, and the other two wouldn't dare. In fact, the other two are probably hiding in their rooms, and perhaps under their beds."

Dr. Tom nodded. "Maria, could you call Trevor as soon as, um, as soon as these proceedings are done, and ask him to come up here to give us a report about what happened? It doesn't seem to me that anything down there is going on by accident." Dr. Tom had never approved of starting fights before, and he would have to communicate to Trevor that "our weapons are not carnal." But at the same time . . . the crowd-work had been masterfully done.

〉〉〉〈〈〈

The one print journalist there was a man with sense enough to keep his distance from the mob. He had been in Beirut and Cairo, and knew that when it came to unhappy crowds, less was more, and more could be learned from a good balcony than from being down in the midst of the fray. He was from the *Post* in the city, and because there was no balcony around, he was leaning nonchalantly against one of the satellite trucks. He was the only one there who noticed what Trevor was doing back by the Whitefield statue, and he took a picture of him with his phone.

Mrs. McCorkadale was up in front, wondering how she had lost control of things. No one was listening to *anything* she said. But to be fair to her, the only other time she had ever had to use a megaphone before was during an exceptionally large tour of the Jefferson Davis Botanical Gardens, that time when the bluebonnets were in.

Suddenly the crowd on the right came into a collective consciousness about what was being yelled at those clean cut kids over there, and the whole group surged into a simultaneous and deep desire to do some hippie punching. That section of the crowd turned to their left and began to move toward the outrage. Sally saw them coming, and she suddenly stopped singing. "Time to scoot, guys," she said, and scoot they did. Those taunting them took momentary satisfaction in their victory, but then turned around to see a surly group of auto mechanics, plumbers, and backhoe operators advancing toward them.

The battle of Choctaw Valley was over in about thirty seconds. The entire left side of the crowd dispersed like they all intended to be somewhere else in five minutes. And the victors stood around for a few minutes more after that, half ashamed of themselves—for hippie punching is never as rewarding as it initially sounds—and then a few said, "Hey, let's get back to the car." That was enough for everybody, and about ten minutes later, the only occupants of the space were Mrs. McCorkadale, two satellite trucks, and a few scattered handfuls of confused people.

3. HIDDEN DEPTHS

TREVOR CAME INTO THE RECEPTION AREA FOR THE president's office, grinning hugely. The morning had turned out *entirely* to his satisfaction. There was a small cut above his left eye, small enough to be incidental, and big enough to be garish, but in an understated way. And he was about to meet Eve, she with the voice. Everything else faded into insignificance.

Dr. Tom, Maria, and Eve were all standing there, waiting for Trevor expectantly. When Maria had called him, he said he would be right up.

As he walked through the door they all fell silent. *What a solid guy*, Dr. Tom thought. *Ouch!* Maria thought. *A hockey player*, Eve thought. This, despite the fact that Trevor had never before in his life seen ice out of doors, unless it was inside a glass of sweet tea.

Dr. Tom stepped forward. "Trevor Smith?"

Trevor nodded his head. "Yes," he said. "Smith. The p is silent."

"Excuse me?"

"Never mind," he said. "Poor joke. Sorry. Lame attempt at literary allusion."

Dr. Tom shook his hand. "Good to meet you," he said. "This is Maria Barancho, my admin assistant, and this is Eve Halliday, her intern this year."

"Pleased to meet all of you," Trevor said. Inside, he was doing spiritual cartwheels. *Eve looks like her voice sounds! And Eve Halliday? This was a sign from Heaven. This was more than fun. This was destiny. This was fun destiny.*

"So," Dr. Tom said. "I see that you have some skills when it comes to crowd dispersal."

"Oh, it was just a little thing that came to me . . . "

"I see. And how did it come to you? What happened?"

Trevor then explained what had happened, emphasizing as much as he could the heroic role played by Eve in obtaining reinforcements, and added one detail that they all had missed because they left their vantage point at the window too early. Because the police had not been informed there was a rally—no permits had been drawn for it—they had been nowhere present. When the fighting broke out, about six people called them and said there was a riot going on at the Bible college. It took them a few moments to find the riot control gear that somebody had stored in the basement, and then they had gone screaming up to the main gate only to find two satellite trucks and a goodish bit of litter. Trevor saw all this through the iron bars of the main gate on his way up to Dr. Tom's office.

"Yes," Dr. Tom said again. "But what gave you the idea in the first place?"

"Well, once in youth group in junior high, our youth pastor went over what Paul did to the Sanhedrin in the book of Acts. 'I am a Pharisee, the son of a Pharisee: in the hope and resurrection of the dead, I am called in question.' We had quite a debate over that. But ever since that moment, I have always wanted to try something like that on a mob. Kind of a bucket list thing."

Dr. Tom laughed, Maria smiled, and Eve just stared.

>>>X<<<

Maria Barancho had been a fixture at Choctaw Valley for some years now, but she was an odd-out sort of fixture. She was a black-haired, brown-eyed Italian in the midst of a bunch of pale Celts who, for some reason, liked to think of themselves as Anglo-Saxons. This is like a German confusing himself with a Frenchman, but the history is admittedly complicated.

Her great-grandfather had left the Roman Catholic church right around the time he had left Italy for New York, and for largely the same reasons. There had been this village priest

in Lombardy who had been more *secular* than a secular cler-
gyman ought to have been, if you know what I mean, but
this only comes into our story by briefly accounting for how
a family of such thoroughbred Italians had become robust
Protestants in the grand tradition of Zanchi—not that they
knew anything about *him*.

When he first arrived in Brooklyn, Calogero Barancho
was greatly helped in finding work (as a brick-layer) by a very
tight group of the Plymouth Brethren he met at a small Bible
chapel he had begun attending, and in addition to all the
pleasant fellowship and good Bible teaching, he was greatly enthused and edified when he discovered all the various
ways of calculating 666 from pictures of the pope's hat. He
passed this general theological outlook on to his five boys,
the youngest of whom—Donato—was Maria's grandfather.
Donato's youngest boy, Girolamo, was Maria's father, who
had met and married Camilla, both of them the age of seventeen, as soon as he had held on to his first real job for a
month. *Good enough*, he thought. *Let's go for it.*

Though Girolamo had been brought up in the strict
ways of his clan, by the time the two of them were in their
mid-thirties, they had mellowed out into a milder form of
ultra-fundamentalism. This is how they had come to send
Maria to Choctaw Valley Bible College—which was about as
liberal a place as you could go (on the Barancho scale) without losing your salvation. She was eighteen at the time, and

she had been living in Choctaw Valley, in one way or another, since that time. She had spent four years getting her degree, then five years working in the college bookstore, and after that had been hired as administrative assistant by Dr. Tom's predecessor. She was cheerful and outgoing, and was very intelligent and competent, but there was a streak of melancholy in there somewhere.

For Maria was a beauty. And she had decided some years before that there was quite possibly an inverse relationship between feminine beauty and feminine happiness. When she first came to Choctaw Valley, it had taken her almost a year to make any friends at all. Most of the boys were terrified of her, and those who weren't scared of her were terrified of what the *other* girls would do if they even talked to her. And needless to say, the girls were usually pretty sullen around her, although in a sweet southern way. All they ever wanted to do whenever they were with her was go to the restroom to check their makeup.

So over those years, Maria had been asked out for coffee precisely three times, by three different guys—two missional pencil-necks and one hypocritical skeezefest—all of whom went promptly out of her life as soon they passed out through the doors of the Starbucks they were in, and good riddance. All in all, she had done a good job guarding her heart, even though no one had ever gotten anywhere close to it. She hadn't needed to guard things *that* intently. To most guys, she was a distant, unattainable majesty, like the slopes of Kilimanjaro.

That is, she had done a good job guarding her heart until about two years before, when she realized one morning with a shock, while brushing her teeth, that she had fallen, and hard, for her boss, Dr. Tom. As best she could figure out, she had done that some weeks before, when he was gone off on vacation visiting his sister in Birmingham, and through a complicated tangle of messed up phone messages back to the office, she had somehow gotten the idea that he had met "someone" there. This had thrown her into a panic, and then there was nothing but high relief when she discovered her error forty-five minutes later. This was a high relief that did nothing but rejoice over the fact that Dr. Tom was still—however unattainable—still technically available. The next morning, while brushing her perfect white teeth, the truth revealed by her manifest and palpable relief over the whole thing came crashing in on her, and so she sat down and acknowledged to herself what was in fact the case. She was a goner.

And he was clueless. High-minded. An office full of thick books. Accreditation visits. Scholarly articles. All of that. Stupid man. Dear stupid, *stupid* man.

This was the very same Maria who buzzed Dr. Tom in his office the day after the almost rally outside the gate. Under her words were hidden depths. "Roland Hedley on line one."

What Roland Hedley—his real name was Martin something, but Maria called him Roland—wanted was permission to film some B-roll for their extensive hour-long flag story at a charity fund-raiser basketball game that night. Dr. Tom was on his guard because their story on the rally that wasn't was not exactly a showcase of fair-mindedness. But after about fifteen minutes of discussion, he reluctantly gave permission. No on-camera interviews, set up in one corner of the gym, get their footage and be done. *Deal?* Deal.

»»×««

This time it was Dr. Tom who left out the unpredictable presence of Trevor on campus.

That evening, forty-five minutes before the charity rumble (a faculty-student thing) was to start, Trevor and a couple of buddies—Max and Timothy—were heading into the gym to help set up a display table. Students and faculty had all pledged a certain amount of money to various ministries and missions in accordance with however many points were scored by their preferred team. Trevor and his buddies were manning the table for Mission Aviation Fellowship. As it happened, their table was located right next to where Dr. Tom had told the camera crew to set up, and that spot was occupied with a stack of tables. "Huh," Martin said. His last name was Malloy. (But to Maria he would always be Roland Hedley.)

Eager to help, Trevor jumped in, "Here, let us move those for you. There will be tables all around the gym. These all have to be moved anyhow." The three of them jumped right on it, and had a spot cleared for the tripod in no time.

"Thanks, guys," Martin said. *You cave-dwellers. You back-of-the-cave-dwellers.*

"Welcome," said Trevor. "Any time." *He seems friendly. But I am not feeling the love somehow.*

"Could you tell me something? One of the things I want to get is the crowd saying the Pledge. You do that before basketball games, right?" *And I bet you also go out into the woodland meadows to try to capture the powers of the air with butterfly nets.*

Trevor glanced up at the American flag displayed on the wall of the gym. "Yeah, I am pretty sure that usually happens . . . Max, is there going to be the Pledge said tonight?" *Still not feeling the love.*

"I'll go check." Max headed off, trotting around the edge of the court to get to the official's table. Max was a straightforward kind of guy, with virtually no interior dialog at all.

"Why do you want to get the Pledge on film?" Trevor asked. *Is it a sin to be this suspicious?*

"We just thought it would be an interesting contrast. College saying the Pledge inside, but not outside, if you see what I mean." *You cornpones.*

Trevor shook his head. "No, I don't know if that is quite right. We are just doing the same thing in different ways. We are subordinating country to God visually outside, and we do it verbally inside. That's why we say 'under God.' It's all the same thing." *Check.*

"How do you figure?" *Man, some of these hill apes think they know how to argue.*

"Well, you all tend to think of the word *God* as a placeholder for some sort of generic divine entity. For us, it is a proper name. Secularists, even the theistic ones, say 'God' and silently add *however you conceive him/her/it to be.* Like it's a neutral, impersonal substance that each person adds their own condiments to in private. But we are using a name. For us, it is just like saying under *Christ.*" Trevor actually did know how to argue.

Martin stopped suddenly. He tried to act like he was considering Trevor's point, but what had happened is that Trevor had just given him an idea. If he got footage of them saying the Pledge of Allegiance, it would be the work of ten minutes to splice in *Christ* instead of *God.* That would really give this Dr. Tom something else to think about. Martin started to get really excited, excused himself from the discussion with Trevor, and spent the remainder of the time checking and rechecking connections, batteries, everything. This was solar brilliance. They wouldn't know what hit them. The entire nation would descend upon these idiots in a high fury.

The remaining twenty minutes crawled by like rapidly cooling magma. Martin Malloy was beside himself with excitement.

When the klaxon finally blew, his fingers were trembling, but only slightly. The crowd quieted—the gym was full—and they all rose. First, they said the Pledge, and Martin moved over to make sure that he had gotten it, and also to turn off the camera until the game started. He would get a few shots in, a few ups and downs on the court, and then back to the studio. But Trevor shouted over from his MAF table, "Wait, there's more!"

Martin stopped, shrugged, and stepped back. The crowd turned away from the flag, clapped three times, and then together chanted the motto of Choctaw Valley Bible College. "No life that's lived for Christ is lost." Then everybody sat down, and the hoop festivities began. Martin was trying not to act giddy. He had the same crowd that said the Pledge saying *Christ*, and he had it on the same tape, and with the same levels. This was going to make the whole thing a snap.

》》X《《

The hour-long story on the flag was going to run the next Friday night, but once Martin showed his producer the doctored footage (without saying anything about its tenuous relationship with what philosophers call the correspondence view of truth), the decision was made to do a three-minute spot the following night.

"Not content with the levels of controversy swirling around his college, Dr. Tom Collins has apparently decided to raise the stakes," Martin said, looking straight into the camera. "Last night at a charity basketball game, the home crowd put their own unique twist on the Pledge of Allegiance. Take a listen." At this cue, Martin looked down and the story cut away to the Choctaw Valley crowd: "I pledge allegiance to the Flag of the United States of America, and to the Republic for which it stands, one Nation under *Christ*, indivisible, with liberty and justice for all."

Back to Martin. *Sweet*, thought Martin. "The college is already embroiled in a huge controversy over the order the flags are in out front of the college. And now this. We do not yet have a comment from the office of the college president, but we will bring it to you when we do."

Martin Malloy was right about the impact that his story would have. The flag story was already hot, and this took the whole thing up to a high summer afternoon on Mercury's bright side, that being the side closest to the sun. And whoever does this sort of thing had a clip of the theocratic Pledge up on YouTube within minutes, and within twenty-four hours it had over two million views. And within two days there were protest rallies in seventeen cities, and the rallies had tens of thousands in attendance.

〉〉〉〈〈〈

Dr. Tom watched the story about twenty times, and he had talked to about twenty people who had been at the game. *He* had

been at the game. *Nobody* had said "under Christ." He supposed
(at least every other time he thought about it) that it would have
been fine with him if they had. But they hadn't. Where did this
thing come from? It had to have been doctored. But how?

He stared at his computer screen malevolently. He was
drafting a press release that numerous outlets were clamoring for, and he wasn't sure whether to play offense or defense.
He didn't want to accuse anybody in particular without evidence, because *did-too-did-not* had never appealed to him.
He stared malevolently at his screen some more.

Maria buzzed him. "Trevor Smith is here to see you."

Dr. Tom brightened. *That* kid might have an idea. "Send
him in."

Tom walked over to his wingback chairs as Trevor walked
in. "Have a seat, have a seat."

"Thank you, sir."

"How can I help you?"

"Well, here's hoping it can go the other way. About that
Pledge story . . .?"

"Yes—you were there, right? *Nobody* said under Christ."

"Right, sir. Nobody."

"Any ideas?"

"Well, it was obviously doctored, and I think we can safely
assert that it had to have been Malloy."

"That's where I am stuck. I am drafting a press release, and
am trying to decide how aggressive to be."

"I think you can be pretty aggressive, sir. Take a look at this." Trevor held out his iPhone, queued up to a video clip. It was some raw phone footage, taken by Trevor's phone, right after the moment when he decided it was not a sin to be suspicious. It was of Malloy's camera set-up, and the entire south-east portion of the bleachers. The crowd was saying the Pledge, and they said it according to Hoyle, and Malloy was standing there recording them as they said it right. Then the phone camera shook as Trevor shouted to him, "Wait, there's more," and Malloy stepped back. Then the crowd said the school motto, and sat down, and Martin Malloy danced a little jig by his camera, and then he sat down. Then the phone stopped.

Dr. Tom's eyes were wide. "Have you done anything with this?"

"This is up on YouTube. So far it has seventeen views. But, to be fair, I think most of those are my mom and my sisters. Here's the link if you want it."

"Want it? *Want* it? Mr. Smith, I am *greatly* in your debt." Dr. Tom wrote down the link, and stood up to return to his computer. "Aggressive it is. But let us just remember what Mark Twain said about how a lie can get halfway around the world while the truth is still putting on his shoes. The Internet has not changed this or made us smarter. It just moves our ignorance around the world at very high rates of speed."

Trevor stood up to go, and Dr. Tom walked him to the door. "What is your take on the lay of the land out there?"

"You mean in the student body?"

"Right, that's what I mean," Tom said.

"Permission to speak freely, sir?"

Dr. Tom laughed. "Yes," he said. "Just like in the war movies."

"Well, the student body is divided about this flag issue—about a third are humiliated by the whole thing, having been taught and unduly influenced by Dr. Jake Rollins. About a third are supportive, but still embarrassed, and about a third are rowdy and enthusiastically in your corner. I am the un-elected liaison to this last faction, numbering, I would guess, about eight hundred souls."

"Thanks," Dr. Tom said. "This enthusiasm you speak of… is it the carnal kind, the zeal of Jehu? Or something else, something I can be less nervous about?"

4. ATMOSPHERIC CRACKLE

MUSTAFA GLARED AT HIS COMPUTER SCREEN. HE had just returned from a most unsatisfactory meeting with Musheer down at the mosque. Some assistant to the imam *he* turned out to be. *"Keep our heads down. Don't stir anything up. Let the infidels sort this one among themselves." Fine, be like that. Coward.*

He clicked view again and watched the unbelievers declaring America to be under Christ. Arrogance! He had hinted darkly to Musheer that there were plenty of young men who felt as he did, and this was no idle comment. He must know a hundred, and they all knew people. He rocked back and forth in his chair trying to figure out what to do. Choctaw Valley was too far away to organize anything there, and there was no representative here in Dearborn . . . Mustafa stopped rocking. If there was no representative here, why not just pick one? Why not just *appoint* one?

Suddenly he sat up straight on the edge of his chair and started clicking through to a local news web site. He thought he remembered seeing some sort of "rally for the flag" notice in the sidebar of one the stories he had read earlier. After a few minutes, he found it again, and checked the time and place carefully. Then he looked up the address of the plaza where they were all going to gather. Then he zoomed out and looked at the surrounding businesses. On one side of the plaza were businesses of the faithful, and on the other were *dhimmi* businesses. This was perfect.

The next morning, 10:00 sharp, about two thousand citizens of Dearborn were gathered in the plaza, waving flags and carrying placards. A makeshift stage was up front, with a lectern, an unfortunately chosen microphone that spazzed out a lot, and a fifteen-foot sign stretched across the back of the stage—Save our Flag! A few cops were ranged around the perimeter of the crowd, but they knew this kind of event. Usually the crowds at this sort of thing said *please* and *thank you* to them, and picked up their own trash. In short, the handful of cops were ill-prepared for what was gathering one block south of the plaza.

What was gathering there were about two hundred friends and acquaintances of Mustafa. They were all assembled in a back room warehouse of one of Mustafa's brothers, and they were all armed with pockets full of rocks, as per instructions. On the other side of the plaza, among the *dhimmi* merchants, there was a van parked halfway down the block that was full of half-gallon gas cans, filled with gas.

Mustafa stood on a box in front of the men (and boys), gestured to them all, and when they quieted down, said a few words. He outlined the plan, and concluded with a shouted *Allahu Akbar!* They all responded in kind, and streamed out the warehouse doors that emptied into the alley, ran up the alley to the main drag, and then sprinted down the block toward the plaza. They were instructed to make no noise until the first of them hit the crowd, and then to start screaming as they pleased. The whole thing unfolded flawlessly. As soon as they reached the edge of the crowd, the middle of the crowd gave way before them, and they began throwing their rocks to the right and left.

The crowd was largely made up of middle-aged men and women, some young moms with strollers, a handful of military men. In short, they were not prepared at *all* for battle. The wedge of young radicals went through the middle of the crowd like a meat cleaver going sideways through a stick of butter. The noncombatants in the crowd scattered, disappearing down side streets, alleys, and into shops.

On the left side of the crowd, the side closest to the stage, the crowd was almost entirely gone within minutes. On the far side of that end a group of young men had banded together and were trying to rummage up some ammo rocks to return fire with. In the middle, in front of the lectern, about the only ones left were the honor guard from a nearby ROTC unit that had been assigned to the event. There were five young cadets, three with flags and two with rifles (with bayonets) and no ammo. One of them had suggested that they make a discrete exit to their car, which was parked behind the stage, but the cadet with the American flag said there was no way he was going anywhere. They had been told to hold a flag at this event until eleven, and that was what he was going to do. Rocks were now falling around them—one bounced off the lectern and hit the state flag cadet on the shoulder. With that, the two cadets with bayonets decided to charge. "Somebody needs to go to the hospital," one of them said. "I think it should that one there with the curly hair." And he took off, the other bayonet right behind.

The flag-bearers followed hard after them. But the rock-throwers were not as plentiful as they had been. About twenty of them were in a melee with the resisters over on the far side, the kind of melee that does not require ammo. About twenty of them were still in the center of the plaza throwing rocks at the remaining people bunched up around the perimeter. And the rest had streamed down the far street toward the van with the gasoline, according to the plan.

When the bayonet charge got close to the remaining rock-throwers, they turned and ran. But one of them had tarried just a little too long, wanting to unload his very last rock, and as he ran he felt a piercing pain in the back of his left thigh, and he went down. He was a garrulous sort, going by the name of Abdul, and his garrulity would serve him well over the next few days. He was going to give many interviews from his hospital bed, and would utter many recriminations about the theocratic crackdown on peace-loving Muslims that was clearly underway. It was all part of a grand strategy—first the *under Christ* Pledge outrage, and now the violent repression of any who would express responsible dissent.

Down the street, on the other side of the plaza, the rioters had whipped open the back of the van, divided up the gas cans, and then ran down the street, breaking in shop windows, dousing the most flammable goods with gasoline, and torching them. When they had about twenty shops well ablaze, Mustafa blew a whistle he had with him, and they all scattered, in every direction.

>>><<<

Peter Kramer had presciently warned Dr. Tom of the possibility of showing up in a photo with a questionable wench on each arm. Kramer was warning against behaving in such a way as to not be photographed in such circumstances, which is to say, don't *do* that—but there are other things to watch out for, as well.

In these postmodern times of ours, it is not necessary to actually be there when such events occur. What does it mean, exactly, to *be* anywhere? What is presence in a particular place but a way of paying homage to certain tired out Cartesian categories? To be in thrall to the Enlightenment? These were issues that Dominic Strabo had often wrestled with as a philosophy major at Ball State, but now, in that his library fines did not prevent his graduation, he did not wrestle with them at all in his current position as assistant editor for the gossip site Jezebel.

It seemed like a stroke of genius at the time, which was about three a.m. He had been out earlier drinking with some friends, and when he got home he had been looking at some, um, photos on the Internet, and when he came to one of them that seemed particularly ripe, he thought of Dr. Tom Collins. Dominic, like so many others of the tolerant tribe, had been regularly and routinely filled with righteous hatreds at the very thought of Collins. And when he looked at that picture, he suddenly wished he had a photo of Collins in the midst of that orgiastic fray. And then, on a whim, he clicked through a few Google images of that decent and kind college president, found a suitable one, masked and filtered it, and spit–spot, as Mary Poppins would say, he had the very photo he had wished he'd had earlier. Even during his days as an undergraduate, his grasp of what could possibly have been meant by the aforementioned correspondence theory of truth had been tenuous.

He put it up on Jezebel, and was quite gratified, upon awakening the next morning, to see that MSNBC and HuffPo had both thought that his news from three a.m. was truly newsworthy. They had posted it also.

〉〉〉✕〈〈〈

Dr. Jake Rollins didn't have any classes this term until after lunch. So he came into the office a little bit late, got himself situated, and rolled through his basic websites. A New Testament scholar cannot hope to stay abreast of the current doings unless he stays abreast of them, if you follow what I mean here. He would grade his papers in a minute. He got to the MSNBC site at about nine twenty a.m., and was sitting in Tom Collins's reception area by about nine forty.

Maria had gone in to see if Dr. Tom was willing to see him, which he was, but only if he could wait ten minutes while Tom finished up a phone call. Maria delivered the message back, and Dr. Rollins said that he could wait. Maria went back around to her chair behind the desk, and looked across at Dr. Rollins balefully. The view was much less appealing than it would have been had Rollins been looking at her, which he wasn't. He was looking carefully at his fingernails which were, truth to tell, perfectly groomed. He would move his hand in the sunlight that streamed in through the window, and look at his right hand from different angles. At one time during his wait, it looked to Maria that he might be trying to see his own reflection in them.

She had the kind of personality that enabled her to like virtually everyone, and whenever she met anybody with whom this superpower was absent, it usually threw her completely. She didn't know how to behave, or where to look. She couldn't just "be herself," because she had no internal directions for this emotional state. She didn't know how to compose her face, and imagined (falsely) that her lip was constantly curled, revealing an antagonistic incisor. She did not know why, but she had felt this way about Dr. Jake Rollins from about two minutes after she had first met him. He was the only permanent fixture on campus who did this to her, and she was ordinarily very grateful that they crossed paths so rarely. He sitting across from her for fifteen minutes straight was about to cause Maria to experience a dark night of the soul.

She kept looking down at the top of her desk in order to pray for grace. Then she would drum her fingers silently. Then she would try to work on the program she had been running earlier that morning. Then she would look at the top of her desk again. She went to the restroom once and ran cold water over the backs of her hands.

After interminable eons, Tom appeared in the doorway of his office, and smiled. He didn't appear to have any problems with Jake. "Hi, Jake," he said warmly, and they both disappeared into the office. Maria stared after them, marveling at the paragon of saintliness who had just greeted Rollins the Insufferable with warmth and kindness, and had apparently meant it.

But while he had no troubles with Jake, the same spirit of collegial *bonhomie* was not exactly returned. Jake Rollins had been a finalist for the position of president of Choctaw Valley, in the last cut alongside Tom. And Rollins had thought, given the credentials *he* brought to the table, that the job was certainly his. It ought to have been.

Jake Rollins had only been two years behind Dr. Tom in their doctoral studies at the University of St. Andrews. They were both stellar students in a stellar theological program (if you don't count all the unbelief and apostasy), but there were striking differences between the two men. A first-rate education had gone *into* Dr. Tom's head, while it had apparently just gone straight *to* Dr. Jake's.

But on paper, Rollins had reasons for his confidence. When it came to the formal credentials, and the number of publications, and the post doc work at Oxford, Rollins had it all over Collins. The thing was a shoe-in. He was Haman getting ready for the banquet of the big time, egged into buying a nice tuxedo by his wife. But unfortunately for his plans, the search committee had four of its five members who would suffer the same kind of visceral reactions to him that Maria suffered.

So when Rollins had lost out to Dr. Tom, of all people, from that time on, whenever Dr. Rollins came into a room where Dr. Tom was, the spiritually sensitive could always pick up on a little atmospheric crackle. Dr. Rollins carried more envy around inside his rib cage than you could find at a drag show in San Francisco. And on this occasion, as Jake walked into Tom's office, you didn't need to be spiritually sensitive to notice it. You could set your iPhone out on the desk, and it would charge all by itself.

"How can I help you?" Tom was jolly, and completely at ease. For some reason, around Jake, he always was.

"I take it that you haven't seen MSNBC yet." Rollins was trying to keep from sneering, and not very successfully.

"No, no," Tom said, getting up and walking over to his computer. In a couple of clicks, he was there. "Land of Goshen!" he said. That was the oath he reserved for moments of extraordinary provocation. "Excuse me just a minute," he said, walking to the door. He opened it slightly, and stuck his head out.

"Maria, could you call Don Carpenter? Have him come up here right away? While he is on his way up, take a look at MSNBC and then turn it off again. Don't stare at it. I'll want a press release asap saying that the photo is doctored. Either

I was not where those people were, or they were not where I was. I am entirely good with either option. Thanks. I'll go over it with you as soon as you have a draft. Thanks."

He closed the door, and walked back to Rollins, and sat down again.

"So you are saying that this was *not* you?" The incredulity in Rollins's voice had already gotten to tremolo levels.

"Right. Not me. They abandoned clean play and sportsmanship in the first quarter. Just amazing."

"So you are just going to deny it, and expect everyone to just believe you?" Rollins had studied, and been affected by, some of the same thinkers that had so shaped the outlook of Dominic Strabo. Simple denials seemed to him to be so old school, and so dependent on naive views of truth, and—not incidentally—filled with contempt for marginalized voices. How anybody like Rollins could have gotten hired at a fundamentalist joint like Choctaw Valley would have been a mystery to anyone who was privy to his views. But since he kept his views entirely out of sight, except at the right conferences, it wasn't that big a mystery after all.

"Well, I don't know what I expect other people to do," Dr. Tom said. "But I know what I am going to do. I am going to laugh at the jitney slander. Give it the raspberry. Maybe two raspberries." Tom noticed, with some surprise, that he had moved from the periodic condition of being fine with a fight into a state of mind that actually wanted to fight.

Rollins just stared in disbelief. "Well, Dr. Collins," he said, becoming suddenly formal, and full of starch. "I can scarcely believe this. This is a tragedy for the college. A *tragedy*." He got up to go, and Dr. Tom walked him to the door.

Tom noticed certain sentences forming in his throat unbidden. He wanted to say, "Really appreciate your work for the college, Jake." But that wasn't diplomatic, it was false. So he didn't say it. But the niceness gears inside were going to have their way about *something*, and so Tom extended his hand to a very reluctant Jake Rollins, and clapped him on the shoulder going out. *Why do I do that?* he wondered, turning back into his office.

⟫⟫)(⟪⟪

Don Carpenter had pulled up a chair next to Maria's desk, and was clicking his teeth with a mechanical pencil. He was staring at the first draft of Maria's press release, thinking hard. Tom was standing back a few feet, thinking just as hard.

Carpenter had arrived just when Rollins was leaving, and before getting to work had beckoned Dr. Tom to come up the hallway with him for just a minute, moving just out of earshot.

"Happy to help with this, Tom, happy to help. But as I think you know, I never want to be found blowing sunshine at anybody, so . . . man-to-man, nothing here? Nothing to it? Just tell me, and I'm fine. You're not going to hang me out to dry, right?"

Tom shook his head. "Nothing to it, Don."

Don was good for his word, and turned around instantly and headed back to Maria's desk. Maria knew what kind of character Don was, and how much of a stickler he was for not doing what's not done, and so she knew *exactly* what he was asking Dr. Tom. She saw Tom shake his head *no* out of the corner of her eye, but it wasn't until she looked up and saw Tom's wide grin as Don was turning and walking away that she was completely reassured. It was a grin full of no guilt and no guile.

So now the three of them were gathered around Maria's desk, all making suggestions and counter-suggestions, when Eve walked in. Her internship was structured around her classes, and she had just gotten out of music. As if in evidence of this, she came in still humming a Celtic version of Psalm 84. Her singing voice was several notches above the one that Trevor had fallen in love with on the phone, and when he heard her singing her solo part on this one at the end-of-term concert, he was going to auger in. Eve was a little bit more than dimly aware of the effect she was having on him, but she didn't mind. Some of it was on purpose.

In the five minutes it had taken her to walk from the music building to the president's office, she had gotten about five text messages from different friends, the last three of them referencing a scathing beatdown of the photo and its source performed, for some reason, by some commie in Portland. As she was coming up the stairs, she had accessed ScuzzWIRED for the first time in her life, and read the top post there with interest and amusement. It had been shared on Facebook somewhere north of 100K times. This was hot property.

When she came into the reception area, Maria came over to tell her what they were doing, and to put her to work on something else. In silent reply, Eve just held up her phone. Maria took about two minutes to read through it, and then walked back over to her desk. "Never mind," she said to Tom and Don.

She then sat down and headed over to MSNBC and HuffPo, and the slanderous apparition had gone all away from both places. "Well, it looks to me as though we need to adjust our press release accordingly, simply saying that we are grateful that the slanderous photograph has been exposed for what it was."

Don said, "And we need to say something about how responsible news outlets need to be more careful and responsible, responsible vetting, etc. Call upon them to set the record straight, etc."

Tom nodded. "Great. And because it appears that this no longer a high wire act, I will just leave you all to it. I still have my remarks for the board I am trying to write. Just run it by me when you are done."

Maria nodded also, tucking her hair behind her right ear like she always did. Tom headed back to his office, wondering momentarily why he had noticed that.

Earlier that morning, the editor of previously introduced ScuzzWIRED had been staring at the screen in disbelief. His name was Montaine Jacobs, which usually embarrassed him, and so he just went by Em. He was up in his office, which was high in the rafters of an old Portland warehouse. He got to it by means of a rope ladder he bought off an old fishing trawler that he found one time in a maritime salvage yard. There was a cat-walk around the edges of the warehouse for the less adventur-ous secretaries. He liked it up there. If hipsters had eyries, his would be the one at the very tippy top. Better than Gwaihir's.

His fingers clattered on the keyboard, and they would only stop when *he* stopped, and he would only stop to say some-thing like *oh, for the love of Mike* to himself. In a small win-dow in the upper left hand part of his screen, he had the pho-to that had just gone up about a half hour before on MSNBC's web site, followed by The Huffington Post. He wasn't sure, but from disturbances in the force he thought that Salon must be thinking about it.

Now hipster editors trying to live out the AdBusters dream don't issue press releases. That wouldn't fit with the vibe. But they do tweet, and they do put up blog posts that deconstruct things like a house was burning down, and they do bust the chops of cyberninnies, which is what Em was currently oc-cupied in doing.

It was the same photo that Tom and Don and Maria had been sweating over. The photo in question represented Tom

Collins at a party that clearly had dubious credentials and points of origin. His right arm was around the shoulders of a floozy-tart without very many clothes on, and his left arm around the waist of a buxom personage who had no clothes on at all. His right hand held a bottle of beer, tipped at a rakish angle. In the background there were other citizens of Babylon doing the sorts of things one might do upon such an occasion. *Oh, for the love of Mike*, Em muttered again. It had taken him about two minutes to find the smiling original of the photo of Dr. Tom on Google Images, where that pious gentleman had been earnestly involved in dedicating the new library of CVBC. And the only female within fifteen feet of Dr. Tom on *that* occasion was the doubtful entry of Dr. Tom's future adversary, Mrs. McCorkadale. And there was no beer of any description anywhere.

The title of Em's post, soon to go viral, was "C'mon, Man . . ."

First he posted the incriminating picture. Then he put up the duddy library shot, with Dr. Tom holding ribbon-cutting scissors instead of a beer bottle. Then he had a couple of boxes where you could drag either picture on top of the other one to show that they indeed displayed a man grinning the very same identical grin, with the same wisp of hair hanging down on his forehead.

Beneath the photos, Em's critique ran as follows.

> We're atheists, too, you know. We want Collins to
> go down as much as anybody. But c'mon, man,

> you're embarrassing us. This photoshop work must
> have been done with scissors stolen from a kinder-
> gartner, along with some library paste taken from
> the teacher lady. And while I am on the general
> subject, that Pledge of Allegiance edit job at KMOZ
> must have been done with a pair of hedge clippers
> that hadn't been oiled for six years . . .

Within fifteen minutes of him posting this, both MSNBC
and HuffPo pulled the offending photo, HuffPo with an
apology. (MSNBC just kept on going, in a state of Zenlike
serenity, like nothing had ever happened.) And later that afternoon, Martin Malloy was summarily sacked by the president of the television station, and, while it has very little to
do with the thread of our larger narrative, he did eventually
become a teacher of journalism at Behemoth. He later married the niece of the judge in the infamous flag desecration
case, referenced earlier, but that doesn't have much to do
with anything. We will just pass on.

Within half an hour after HuffPo apologized to the
world, Em got a very gracious email from a woman named
Maria Barancho.

"Dear Mr. Jacobs," it began.

> Dr. Collins asked me to write in order to pass on
> his personal thanks for your integrity in this mat-
> ter. A glance at your site indicates that we are not
> exactly walking the same path, but your efforts to

stomp out incompetent slander are appreciated just
the same.

Cordially, etc.

Em thought that was nice, and absentmindedly clicked
on the profile picture next to Maria's email, and jumped in
his seat. *Yikes*, he thought. *How do the fundamentalists rate
such beauties?*

5. A CULTURE OF INTIMIDATION

A LONG MAHOGANY TABLE FILLED ONE SIDE OF THE large conference room. Facing the side of that table, in four long rows of chairs, a gallery had been established. The carpet was a rich burgundy color, and the wainscot around the room was a nicely matched cherry. The room was solemn, elegant, dignified, and not ready for the meeting that was about to happen in it.

The special board meeting called to address the "matter of the flag" began with Dr. Tom summarizing what had happened, how it all had come about, and how he saw the Lord's hand in it. He then moved on to what he saw as the theological issues, the political issues, and the possible impact the controversy might have on the mission of the college. His presentation took about fifteen minutes, and didn't embarrass the room at all.

"There is a practical aspect to all this, which I will let Don address," he said. "But as far as our place in the world goes, we are attracting some hostility we don't want *and* some hostility that I think we do want, as well as attracting some support we don't want along with a significant amount that we do. There is always something."

As Tom intimated, the second item on the agenda was Don Carpenter's report on the stupendous improvement in all their numbers—donations and applications for enrollment both. He spent a few minutes passing around some last-minute pie graphs and comparisons, sheets with bottom lines on them, and sheets that didn't have anything but numbers.

"What has happened," he concluded, "is somewhat counterintuitive. Some might have expected a flood of controversy like this to damage our . . . testimony." He remembered just in time that Dr. Tom hated the word *brand*, and so he veered at the last minute over to *testimony*. Tomayto, tomahto.

"If you look at your notebooks under the third tab, I have included a few representative letters and notes. These were letters attached to checks, one of them in six figures. So I will simply note for the record that we are being called a lot of names, both good and bad. But the people calling us the *good* names are writing us some pretty hefty checks."

Don stopped, and scratched his cheek reflectively. "Moving on to recruitment, I was just in John's office this afternoon, getting his latest numbers. He says that he has never seen anything like it, and he has been working for us in that position for fifteen years. Requests for applications are way up, something like sixty percent. So there you have it. Any questions?"

There were none, so Don walked thoughtfully—he always walked thoughtfully—over to his seat in the gallery, which contained a number of observers from the college community. Maria was in the front row, and she was doing well spiritually because she had not seen Dr. Jake Rollins come in, and he was seated straight behind her, two rows back.

The first returns were running strongly in Tom's direction, but the next thing to happen was the reading of several letters addressed to the board. This by itself would not be a big deal, except for the fact that they were letters from the governor, two senators, and the chairman of the Republican National Committee. The letters did not expressly mention, but implied strongly, that the issues at stake involved the survival of mom, apple pie, and the red-checked tablecloth on the kitchen table. The letters were agonizingly full of patriotic treacle, but were no less effective for all that. Kramer had trouble reading them aloud, though, and had to fight down the constant impulse to wad the letters up and throw them across the room. But he refrained. "I read them aloud as requested," he said when done, "but there are copies provided for you in the notebook."

Silence fell over the room. Peter Kramer looked down at
his agenda, and the next item was "Faculty Request to Address
the Board." He looked up, saw that Dr. Rollins was, in fact,
present, and called his name. Maria's heart sank. She was not
at all spiritually prepared for this. She was unprepared for it,
and she had to stay to see what was going to happen. She
should have known. Of course he was going to be here. She
didn't know why she had overlooked such an obvious thing.
She was still spiritually unprepared. Maybe she wanted to be
spiritually unprepared.

Dr. Rollins walked around to the same place where Don
Carpenter had been. A small lectern was there for any non-
board member (other than Tom) who was invited to address
the board. He walked up with his head bowed, and he had a
grim, settled smile as he went. Maria scrunched down in her
seat, and started quoting Bible verses at herself.

She was doing pretty well until about three minutes into
his presentation. He gestured expansively, with the kind
of gesture that he had found so effective in the impressing
of freshmen girls, and Maria almost lost it. His right hand
moved languidly toward the ceiling, and Dr. Rollins was un-
able to keep himself from looking at it as it went. The board
members, being all men, didn't notice, but Maria did, and
started biting her forefinger.

"We are called to be all things to all men . . . poor testimony . . . laughingstock at SBL . . . the first will be last . . . build

bridges, not walls . . ." Dr. Rollins was walking a fine line, and he knew it. He was using some of the standard phrases he had picked up from some of his friends at the more . . . *open* conferences that he went to, but only the phrases that he did not believe the board members would recognize. They would react to liberal jargon, but not, he hoped, to the liberal bent decked out in the very latest jargon. He thought he saw empathy in the eyes of more than a few of the board members. But no one said anything, so he was still left unsure.

"As an emissary from the New Testament department," Dr. Jake Rollins said, "I am afraid that unless this situation is addressed in a satisfactory way, I—along with a number of my colleagues—will likely resign our positions if Tom is kept on."

Two birds with one stone, thought Kramer. *Win the flag battle, and clean out a festering department.*

But one of the other board members, a man named Michael, was apparently more in touch with his charitable impulses.

"You say 'a number of your colleagues,'" he said. "Others feel the way you do?"

"Yes," he said. "I have talked to quite a few who are quite concerned about this."

Oldest trick in the book, Tom thought. *Take a secret ballot and announce the results . . . bet he won't tell us who. Invisopolling at its finest.*

"Do you mind saying who might join you?" Mike asked.

"Well, I would, but I feel that it would be a violation of Christian charity. And more than a few of them have alluded to the culture of intimidation that exists in our administration-faculty communication."

Oooo! Maria thought. *Culture of intimidation? Tom? He was a perfect baa-lamb, and not intimidating at all. Well, actually, he was intimidating if you were secretly in love with him. But not otherwise. Perfectly approachable otherwise.*

The ten members of the board sat solemnly around the table, stacks of paper in front of each of them, along with a couple of notebooks. From looking at their expressions, it was not possible to tell which of them had been on the phone with the governor. Those of them who had been conversing with the governor had had their arms twisted like only a governor can do, and if a governor knows what he is doing—as this one did—it doesn't show. It never shows, not even in the autopsies.

Once comments had been taken from the floor—besides Jake Rollins, only two other people were given permission to speak—the board turned to the question of what to do about what Tom had done both *to* and *for* the college. They were going to have to do something, one way or another. Different motions were put forward, and they were in various states of readiness. Some just rolled out onto the table, looked embarrassed for a moment, and then rolled off again for lack of a second. Others were discussed for ten minutes or so, until everybody saw how lame they were, and were withdrawn. The discussion alternated between exhilarating and tedious. Depending on what was being suggested, Maria switched back and forth between adrenaline rushes and counting the patterns in the carpet.

Finally, one of the board members cleared his throat—his name was Rob—and gruffly said, "Look, I am not saying this is pleasant for anybody, but I want to move that we let Dr. Tom go, with many thanks for his years of service. I don't think we can afford this kind of thing. I so move." This motion, unlike the previous ones, at least had the virtue of clarity, and no one in the room could tell how the thing was going to go from the earlier discussion. They all knew it had a chance of passing. "I'll second that," came another voice from across the table. That's two.

Kramer, secure in his role as the chair, and perched on top of a clean conscience, looked around the table calmly. "All right, gents, glad to have the issue plainly before us. You all ready to vote? We would all like to see how it is going to go, right?"

Several heads nodded grimly. Others were looking at the table.

Kramer continued. "Here's how we are going to vote. This way. Because of the importance of this issue, we will vote silently, using pen and paper. Tear off a scrap piece of paper, and write *dismiss* or *not dismiss* on it."

At that he tore of a piece of paper, scribbled his vote on it, and folded it in half. "Like this," he said.

"Wait a minute," Rob said. "You're the chairman. The chairman doesn't vote."

"Well, actually, he can," Kramer said. "I read through *Robert's Rules* again when this whole thing blew up, and realized that the chairman votes when there is a tie—which everybody knows about—but can also vote when it is not an open voice vote. The chairman doesn't usually vote for the sake of good manners. It is not a matter of law."

"Hold on," Rob said. "That can't be right . . . or maybe it is right. We can just change it, though."

"No," Kramer said, "Our bylaws say that procedural changes like this cannot take effect until the meeting after the one in which they are made. And it is quite emphatic that we are to be governed procedurally by *Roberts' Rules*. And our bylaws also say that in case of a dispute about procedural protocols, the chairman makes the determination. And it seems pretty straightforward to me. I can vote if we are voting this way. And I have the authority to determine how the voting is to be done."

Rob was just staring at Kramer, feeling outgunned and outmaneuvered, and was wondering how he was going to explain this to the governor. He had been very confident earlier that evening on the phone, and had as much as told the governor that he could come over to the college at his convenience and raise the flag himself. With photographers.

Nobody was expecting this move by their chairman, and one of the men who had been flipped by the governor, and who had been feeling queasy ever since, flopped back again—especially since they were voting on scraps of paper without signatures. All the men tore out a sheet from their notebooks, scribbled their votes, and silently pushed them across the table.

Kramer sorted them as they came in, shoving them into two separate piles, out where everyone could see him. There were a number of people in the gallery craning their necks. Six to four, in favor of retaining Dr. Tom. Maria sighed, almost audibly. If not for good old *Robert's Rules*, Tom would have been long gone, five to four.

Looking around the room, Kramer announced loudly, "As this was a specially called board meeting, intended for the purpose of attending to the one item of business for the called meeting, and as we have attended to that business, I declare the meeting adjourned."

Rollins, and a number of the other disgruntled members of the gallery huffed out of a door toward the back. Maria came up to Tom, smiled at him, and said, simply, "I'm very glad."

"Me, too," he said, running his hands through his hair.

After about fifteen minutes of visiting, and receiving congratulations from his well-wishers, most of whom were students, and not New Testament majors, Tom finally decided to head out. It had been a long day. Peter Kramer followed Tom out the door of the boardroom.

"Do you have about ten minutes?" he asked.

"Sure. I have to pick up a few things from the office before heading to the car. We can talk there."

When they got to the office, Tom flipped on the lights, grabbed his brief case, and set it on the floor by one of the wing backs. He gestured to the other chair. "Have a seat," he said.

"Sure, but just for a minute," Kramer said.

"Thanks for all you did in there," Tom said.

"You are most welcome," Kramer said. Then he sat quietly for a moment.

"Look," he said. "I misjudged how hard the bad guys were going to come after you. I told you that you had two years, easy. And I thought I could guarantee it at the time. But this vote tonight was a lot closer than I thought it was going to be. Apparently the governor has been putting the screws on, and he knows where to put them, believe me. The only thing that saved us was that he didn't have time to get to everybody. Stan was on a hunting trip until yesterday, some place with no cell coverage, and Hank was in the Sudan on that mission trip. And the other three are okay, God having been pleased to give them spines. But give the governor enough time, and I think he can flip the board if he can work over our two world travelers. And when they flip, they will think they are obeying Romans 13 or something. It will turn into a matter of high principle."

"So what are you saying? What do you want to do?"

"Me? I want to fight, even if it turns into the Alamo. But it became apparent to me, riding herd on these guys, that this is going to be a tougher game than hardball. Don't get me wrong. I am all in. But . . . I just wanted to let you know that, if *you* bow out, I would try hard not to fault you. You're the one who's gonna be in the crosshairs. You didn't know how high the stakes were gonna get when this all started. I thought it would be a decent thing for me to do, giving you an out, if you wanted it."

"That's true enough," Tom said. "I didn't know the stakes at the start. But I do know now, and now is when God decided to let me know what the stakes might be. Maybe He didn't trust me with that info earlier. But I am in it for the whole ride."

"You sure now?"

"That sounded anti-climacteric. But I am not talking about a kiddie ride at the county fair. I know this is a bull ride at the rodeo. And not eight seconds either. I know I have to stay on until the bull pukes."

Kramer raised his eyebrows.

"I know. When this whole thing started, I knew my job was on the line. But now I think that they are going to try to destroy *me*, somehow, some way. And as I have been thinking about this, I decided it might be better to be a broken man than a man who never risked breaking anything. We don't really play cards here at Choctaw Valley, but you can deal me in."

Peter Kramer grinned a wide and ugly grin, which Tom found strangely reassuring. "Oh, that's great. We don't really do saloon brawls here either, but that is what this is going to be."

"But now you do have me curious," Tom said. "If the governor can just bully the board and flip them like a couple of pancakes, what does it matter what I think, or what you think? We can quote lines from *Braveheart* to each other all night. All they have to do is vote me out."

"Ah, that is where our friend who wrote *Robert's Rules* comes in. I told you in my first visit that I had gone through our bylaws, and our policy manual, and *Robert's Rules*, which are referenced in both the bylaws and the policy manual. I am the chairman, and the way everything is written, the only way we can have a special meeting is if I agree to it, and if I call it. And the next stated board meeting is not for another six months. They can't fire you if they can't meet. And I am here to tell you, Dr. Tom Collins, that the gentlemen who just now adjourned are not going to be in that board room together as a board for another six months. Not going to happen. Not unless I have an accident in the shower. Or my car blows up, like in the movies."

"But we just had a special meeting . . ."

"Right. I called it, like a bozo. I didn't figure this angle out until after I did. But it was also after that that I also found out how much heat was coming from the governor. But we are good for the present."

The two men sat quietly for a moment, silently tapping the arms of the chairs together. Kramer looked up. "Been discovering anything new in your flag research?"

Tom grinned. "I found out that the Church of England has flagstaffs that fly the flag of St. George, along with the diocesan arms if they can. But that doesn't help us here, right?"

"No. No. Not really."

>>>X<<<

Trevor Smith was the scion of a family that had plenty of bucks, but which had somehow managed to keep that fact from rotting out the floorboards of its collective soul. They had money—quite a bit of it, actually—but for them, money was just bullets. Trevor's great-grandfather was the one who had made the first great installment on the mammon pile, and it had only been growing since that time. This, despite the fact that they used most of their ongoing surpluses to fund mission work—supporting several hundreds of missionaries, in Asia mostly. The more they did this kind of thing with their money, the more money they kept finding to work with. Some people cast their bread on the waters, and all they get is soggy bread, or happy ducks. Others were like the Smith dynasty, and nobody quite knew how it worked.

He had a shock of blond hair that was parted almost in the middle, as though someone from the 1920s had taught him how to comb it. At the same time, he looked as though he were doing it somehow on purpose, and it didn't really look out of place. His jaw was firm without being belligerent, and his nose, which had been straight when he first got it, now had a couple of slight cricks in it—one from basketball and one from lacrosse. He walked lightly, in a way that looked as though he would always be hard to surprise.

So Trevor had grown up with an expectation that surrounded all the younger members of his extended clan. It was the kind of family where the young men were expected to go off to school and then to make their own way in the world of great adventures—five years or so was respectable—before coming back home and joining the firm in some useful and productive capacity. They were always expected to come back with a dragon head or two, and it was never looked down on if they came back with a beautiful and exotic woman from Ecuador or something. Trevor's uncle had done that.

Trevor was a senior now, his plan for the last two years had been to become an MAF jungle pilot, and he had just met Eve Halliday. His first thought upon meeting her was that he was way ahead of schedule. He had once heard his grandfather say, in reference to his grandmother, that she was the butterfly's boots, and this was a sentiment that Trevor now thought he understood the deeper meaning of.

He had fallen for her voice—that *voice*!—the day of the rally out in front of the college, and then, when he had actually met her, he had decided within minutes that it would be criminal negligence on his part not to be in hot pursuit. Of course, he must not *look* like he was in hot pursuit. Some girls don't go for that. He ought to look like he was sauntering. Sauntering purposively.

Eve, for her part, was aware of Trevor, for it would be hard for anybody not to be, and she was also partly aware of the fact that he would look at her more frequently and more intently than he looked at others. And Trevor, for *his* part, was no longer aware that there were any others.

Trevor, of course, was extremely hard on himself when he discovered, after they had met formally in Dr. Tom's office, that they actually were taking one class together. How he could possibly have been in the same room with this vision and not known about it was an indication that he was being spiritually dull and lethargic, and was quite possibly backslidden. He resolved to read his Bible and pray more, although he did acknowledge, in his own defense, that it was a big classroom and she would come in through a different door.

But not anymore. Trevor found out right away what door she came through, found out what dorm she was in, and figured out how to cross paths with her accidentally on purpose as they made their way to class. And as it happened, this is what he had just done.

And also, as it happened, this one class they had together was an advanced New Testament survey course taught by, as

the reader has no doubt anticipated, Dr. Jake Rollins. Word
about what Rollins had said at the board meeting two nights
before had spread through the entire student body like wild,
as they say, fire, and quite a number of those coming to class
that day were eagerly looking for Dr. Rollins to say something
about it. He was the kind of teacher who was usually not very
reticent about recruiting disciples to his particular points of
view. Those successfully recruited would sit in the front so
that the girls among them could watch the fluidity of his hand
gestures. He was quite a hand-dancer.

But those who were counting the days until this re-
quired-for-graduation class was over would sit in the back,
muttering. Before this day, Trevor had been in the back left
corner, and Eve in the back right corner, where the light was
bad. However, as has been mentioned already, not any more.
Trevor was now firmly settled in Eve's corner, in the ardent
hope that one day soon, she would be in his.

Dr. Rollins came into the classroom ruffled and frustrat-
ed. He was not a man of high courage really, or principle either, and he had been grievously let down by one of the board
members who had voted for Dr. Tom's ouster. *That* man was
an optimistic and jolly sort of glad-hander, and *his* talk with
the governor had made him think the whole thing was "in
the bag," and he had said as much to Dr. Rollins. Since it
was in the *bag*, Dr. Rollins had thought he could say what he
had said about needing to leave the college if Dr. Tom stayed

on, and so now here he was, just floating out there. To make things worse, the chairman of the board had sent him an email the day after the board meeting indicating that he had taken Dr. Rollins' comments seriously and at face value, and wanted to talk about "transition." Rollins had not yet decided how to answer that one. He didn't have anything lined up. He had no place to land.

Kramer, for his part, knew that Rollins had probably been bluffing. But he wasn't about to let such an opportunity go by, and if Rollins was going to have to climb down, he was going to do it in public, and it wasn't going to be easy. Kramer had noticed that peculiar smell emanating from the New Testament department for years . . . and he didn't even live in town.

So into the classroom Rollins fluttered, all in a doodah. He dumped his Guatemalan leather tote bag on the table in front of him, and dropped the notebook on the lectern, and began flipping the pages in an irritated manner. The class was eerily silent. After a moment, Rollins looked out over his glasses, and said, in his most condescending, professorial manner, "I hope you are all as dismayed as I was by the events of the other night."

The class sat silently. Those in front were hoping for wisdom to slosh all over them. Those in the back were hoping that there would at least be *some* excitement, for this was a class in which excitement did not usually feature very largely. The apostle Paul lived one of the most thrilling lives ever lived, and yet the good professor seemed to have the ability to present the second missionary journey as something at the same level as watching paint dry. If you were under his spell, it was enchanting. If you were not, it was enchanting the same way fifty minutes of tedium was enchanting. But maybe today would be different. Rollins was agitated, and seemed more interested in an actual issue than in watching his own gestures.

Trevor was seated two rows in front of Eve. Far enough away to seem casual but friendly, and close enough to strike up a natural conversation with her after class was over. Easy peasy, double squeezy. Unfortunately, this placement directly in front of his beloved also meant that he was vulnerable to the temptation of showing off, and so when Dr. Rollins asked his next question, Trevor's hand went up almost immediately.

"Is anyone here actually in *sympathy* with this . . . this . . . *quixotic* battle that our president has for some reason chosen to fight?"

Quite a few of the students, at least in the back, were in sympathy with *anything* that irritated their good professor, but they weren't about to say so. Putting it that way seemed so crass, and some of them couldn't afford to risk anything negative happening to their grades. So most of them sat there, but Trevor's hand was up.

"Yes . . . Mr. Smith, is it?"

5. A CULTURE OF INTIMIDATION

Trevor said *yes sir*, like a good Southern boy. A number of heads in the first three rows swiveled around, as though they could scarcely credit it. Someone in this classroom had the temerity . . . is that the word? . . . we think so . . . the *temerity* to challenge the professor? It did not occur to them to wonder why the professor had the temerity to challenge the president. Their loyalties were all locally sourced.

Rollins looked at his notebook. "Well, we do need to get to Lystra and Derbe today, but before doing that . . . Mr. Smith, do you mind telling us why you are in sympathy with the president on this flag issue?"

"Yes, sir, I would be happy to. We are a Christian college, and we confess that Jesus is Lord. He is not simply Lord of a spiritual zone somewhere, but He is Lord of the *nations*."

As he spoke those words, something else occurred to him suddenly, and he made a note to mention it to Dr. Tom. "And that is the thing. In our college chapel, we have the words 'Christ, Lord of the nations' carved in the woodwork above the platform. It seems to me that all Dr. Tom is doing with the three flag poles is simply to demonstrate outside what we have been saying inside for as long as I have been here."

Dr. Rollins just stared at him coldly. He felt like a quarterback who had just been ear-holed by a linebacker with poor manners and a bad attitude. He chewed his lip for a second. "The inscription in the chapel," he began with an unctuous smoothness, "is a *spiritual* truth . . ."

Trevor pressed the point. "My understanding is that if Christ is the Lord of the nations, and that if this nation is one of those nations, then He is the Lord of this one also. If He is the Lord of this one, then His flag should be given precedence by those who actually confess to believe He has that precedence. The only clear way off this point, as I see it, would be to deny that the Christian flag is *His* flag. That would be a reasonable line of argument, it would seem to me."

His professor stammered for a moment, hesitant to take this offered way of escape. It seemed to him like a trap, because it was. So he tried his first line again. "Christ is the Lord of the nations in a *spiritual* sense," he said. A number of ponytails in the front rows bobbed because they saw that this was intended to make sense.

"But what does that even mean?" Trevor asked.

In the past, Rollins liked to use to this line of argument mostly because of what it *didn't* mean, which was the misguided idea that Christ was Lord of the nations in any way that made any practical difference to them. Asked what it *did* mean, in such a point blank way, the sensations he felt were a complete novelty to him. He looked down at the front rows filled with disciples, pens poised above their notebooks, ready to record the answer. He bit his lip, hoping that it looked magisterial.

"When I say that Christ is Lord of the nations in a spiritual sense, I am simply developing what the Lord meant when He said that His kingdom was not of this world . . ."

"We learned from Dr. Henry last week that that passage should more accurately be rendered as His kingdom is not *from* this world, meaning that it is not grounded in earthly principles. Not that it doesn't or can't have any earthly impact on the world."

Dr. Rollins decided it was time to fall back to the way out that was offered him earlier. "You said earlier that you thought a reasonable argument could be made that the Christian flag was not *really* Christ's flag."

Rollins was a master at changing topics in the middle of conversations in a way that looked as though he were merely developing his thoughts, rather than dispensing with some of them.

"Yes sir," Trevor said again.

"And so I think we might be able to agree that when Jesus and the disciples were walking from Galilee down to Jerusalem, they did not assign one of them to carry the flag. And if they had done so, it almost certainly would not have been *this* flag." Rollins smiled a bit, pleased with himself.

"Yes sir, we agree on all that," Trevor replied. "And I doubt if they had a drummer. Or a bugler. Or a fife. And no tricorner hats and heroic poses."

"As we agree it was not Galilee, do you happen to know the origins of this flag?"

"Yes sir, I do." Trevor had in fact read up on the whole thing as soon as the controversy broke.

Dr. Rollins gestured with his hands, as much as to say *go on*, and he was agitated enough that he didn't even notice his hands as he did so.

"The flag comes from Brooklyn. In 1897, a scheduled speaker for a Sunday School didn't show up, and the superintendent, a man named Charles Overton, had to give an impromptu lecture on the spot. He took the basic layout of the American flag, and asked the students to help him devise a Christian flag. They did so, and the whole incident stuck with him. Ten years later, he and another guy named Robert Diffendorfer—which was a little unfortunate—put together the design we now have, and began to promote it. It caught on, pretty much every place except Europe."

"You seem singularly well-informed. Do you have an interpretation of this flag that was cooked up in Brooklyn, two thousand years after the last apostle died?" There was a good deal of tittering in the front rows at this jab.

"Yes sir," Trevor said. "The Latin cross is red, symbolizing the blood of Christ. The blue canton represents the waters of baptism, along with the faithfulness of Jesus. The field is white and refers to the righteousness or purity of Christ."

"And why," Dr. Rollins asked, winding up for the blow that would lay this young fellow low, "should we be using this flag when it had nothing to do with Jesus, or the apostles, and the heraldry of which is specified nowhere in the Bible?" He had suspected a trap earlier, and it would have been good if he had gone on suspecting a trap. But he was annoyed, and so he didn't.

"The reason I think we should be using this flag to represent our commitment to Christ is that it represents a true spirit of international catholicity—one of the things that we in the fundamentalist world have had notable trouble with. This flag is truly and genuinely transdenominational."

In taking these particular words for his reply, Trevor was in fact quoting several of the favorite catch phrases of Dr. Rollins himself, which he had memorized along with a number of his dorm fellows on the night of the "sound like Dr. Rollins contest," which Trevor had won handily, while standing behind an upturned coffee table as a makeshift lectern, in a dorm lobby filled with howling students. (He had brought down the house with the languid fingers thing.) The phrases in question were *true spirit of international catholicity* and *we in the fundamentalist world have had notable trouble with* and of course *transdenominational*. Also, Rollins liked using the term *catholicity* because, in the world of Choctaw Valley Bible School, that made him something of a bad boy and a renegade.

Dr. Rollins recognized his words in what Trevor had just said. *Check*, he thought. *Let me think about it.*

Trevor replied with a simple *Mate. Take your time.*

Rollins continued to stare for a moment. "Perhaps we can pick this up next time. We really need to get on to Lystra."

Fifty long minutes later, Trevor and Eve were walking slowly down the walk together and, as Trevor had arranged, apparently by accident.

"Good job in there," Eve said.

But Trevor's conscience was bothering him. "I do kind of feel bad about that," he said. "If you asked me point blank about it, I would have to admit that I was showing off."

Eve was shrewd enough not to ask who he was showing off for, and so she just continued walking.

"I was showing off," Trevor repeated. "Spiritual pride," he added, trying not to be proud of his humility.

"Well," Eve said, "that *does* mean you lost your treasure in Heaven. And that is not ideal. You should try harder in the future to not do that. But I still enjoyed it."

6. MONEY TROUBLES

MARIA LOOKED QUIZZICALLY AT THE ELDERLY GEN-
tleman who was sitting in her reception area, and buzzed
Dr. Tom. He certainly looked like a nice man. If he had *not*
looked like a nice man, Maria would have naturally fulfilled
her role as one of the best gatekeepers in the business. But he
looked like a nice man, which counted for a lot with Maria,
and so she buzzed Dr. Tom.

"A Mr. Akroyd to see you," she said. "He's not on the cal-
endar, but your ten thirty called a few minutes ago and had to
cancel. Would you like to see him?"

Dr. Tom was feeling curious that morning, and said *sure,
why not.* He also knew that whenever Maria asked if it was
okay, it was going to be okay. She was a very good judge of

who was going to be a nice person. He noticed yet again, albeit fleetingly, how much he relied on her judgment.

Anthony A. Akroyd, for that was his name, got up slowly, brushed several gray beard hairs off his blue jacket, and walked through the door indicated by Maria. He was about sixty, but his time in the Alaskan oil fields had made him seem about ten years older than that. "Thank you so much," he said, as he went through. His voice sounded like loose gravel being stirred by a stick.

Tom met him at the door, where they shook hands and exchanged names. Tom gave his name, and Anthony said, "Call me Trip." Tom's eyebrows went up, and Anthony, now Trip, said, "Anthony Albert Akroyd, known to my friends in the field as Triple A, and then finally, in the interests of economy, Trip."

This explanation was satisfactory, and so after those initial interactions, Tom escorted him over to the armchairs. Maria appeared at Mr. Akroyd's left elbow as he was sitting down, and asked if he would like some coffee or some water. "Water, please," he said. Maria wondered what was going to happen when his gravel got wet. The answer, as it turned out, was not much.

"I'll have some too, Maria, thank you." Tom said.

Tom and Trip exchanged pleasantries while Maria was getting them their drinks, and when she pulled the door closed behind her, Tom opened the discussion up.

"So how can I help you?"

"Well, you'll pardon me if I state my business directly? Come straight to the point? I don't want to take up your time unnecessarily."

"I would appreciate any directness you might want to send my way. But the time isn't the problem. Just call me curious."

"I have been up in Alaska my whole life, with only occasional trips down to the lower forty-eight. To be frank, I have been discouraged more often than not by how little you all down here seem to resist the constant encroachments on our liberties, or even to *see* those encroachments. But then occasionally, somebody does something kind of out there, like you, and that bucks me up again."

"Well, thank you."

"And here is the weird thing. I don't *agree* with what you are doing at all. I wouldn't do it myself. That flag thing would never have occurred to me. And the God part of it . . . depending on my mood and what day of the week it is, I don't always believe in God. Not sure about that part at all. But the people who are ticked off at what you are doing are all the same people that any honest man should want to find on the other team. Over *there* with the bad guys. And so it is that I find myself really wanting to be on your team."

"So the enemy of your enemy is your friend? That kind of thing?"

The old man shook his head. "No, not exactly. It is more like, 'If *that* guy is the enemy of *those* guys, then he clearly has a lot more going for him than Bible college presidents usually do.' No offense. So it is not quite that we are cobelligerents—I have a lot of respect for what you are doing."

"Well, thanks again," Tom said. "And so . . .?"

"I have been privileged to make a bit of money in my time, though I had to spend more time out in the cold to do it than I would have liked. But now I have a nice place in Anchorage, so it all turned out good. Got a real nice fireplace. Now I just look at spreadsheets, and tend to my foundation. And sit by the fire."

Tom sat quietly because it felt like Trip was coming to the point. Trip, for his part, sat for a moment, and then picked up the thread again.

"As I watched the gaudy uproar in the news about your flag business, it occurred to me that you were a man who very soon was going to have all the trouble in the world. I have been up against these thugs before, some with different names, and some with the same names. Remind me sometime to tell you a story about your governor and the oil drilling equipment fiasco. He got a cool half million out of that one. I was in college with him, down in Idaho. He was on the make from the first day I met him freshman year, which means he was probably on the make before that. I don't think *I* caused it. He was a bad man then, but of course he had not fully ripened. I never saw such a lia— . . . but I am getting distracted. Not only do these people know how to bust your kneecaps, they know how to do it in a way that makes all the major media acclaim them for their altruistic zeal to save the children. They always want to do it for the children. But they never do, turns out, and the children go home crying, not having received the candy they were promised." He paused. "Metaphors get away from me. Sorry."

Tom arched his eyebrows. "So you are saying that I might be in some personal danger?"

"I could almost see a red laser pointer dot quivering right next to your tie tack."

Tom grinned, in spite of himself. *Now why would that be funny?*

"But they never *start* there. They are smart enough to work up to it. They are fastidious enough to bleed all your money before trying to bleed anything so crass as your blood. And *smart* enough to do it that way too. I only saw this kind of critter lose his cool once. Now when he did, it was well worth the wait, and he made about twenty mistakes in a row because of it. That was when I got my half mil back, and then some. But they almost never lose their cool."

Dr. Tom nodded. "You have my attention. Go on."

"And so I said to myself—talking to myself was a habit I got into out on the north slope—Trip, that nice man is going to have all the trouble in the world. Why don't we see to it that money troubles are not part of it?"

"I don't understand." Tom sat up in a chair a little straighter, and more than a little awkwardly. Talking about money with donors was the least favorite part of his job as president, and here it had crept up on him unexpectedly.

"I want to leave this little checkbook with you—from my foundation. If you sign this paper here, it will make you a signatory on this one account. I have that part all arranged with the bank. You can have your administrative assistant out there—sweet girl, by the way—email a PDF of the signed paper, here to this address. The lady on the other end is named Debbie, and she is expecting it. I have dealt with her for years. You would be preauthorized to spend up to five million."

"Five *million*!? What on earth would I have to do to spend five million on this?"

Trip chuckled, and shook his head. "I told you . . . I have been into multiple fraca— . . . what's the plural of fracas? Don't know, but I have been in a bunch of them before with these . . ." He stopped, remembering just in time that he was on the grounds of a Bible college, "these . . . rapscallions," he finished.

Tom was just staring at him. *Five million.*

Trip picked up the thread again.

"Look. They know how to make you really burn through that stuff. And their first and second rounds usually consist of threats to bankrupt you. You have finite pockets, and they want you to know it. And they also want you to believe that *their* pockets are as deep as the all-round generosity and goobyness of the American taxpayer. Which is, let us be frank, pretty deep on both counts. During those initial assaults of theirs, I would like *you* to have the knowledge that you have some check-signing abilities. And I would like them to be wondering where your serene inner peace was coming from. Besides from the Holy Spirit."

"Well," Tom said. "I am very grateful for your generous— and entirely unexpected—offer. I will promise you that I will think and pray about it. But before signing *anything*, I would need to have some of my people do some checking—references, the background of your foundation, and so on. I am sure you understand. No offense. I have some friends up that way I can ask."

Trip smiled. "I could ask you who they might be, but it is best that you check with them without my knowing any of their names. You can tell me later if you want."

"So you understand my caution?"

Trip laughed out loud. "Oh, I understand it perfectly. In fact, you just passed the first test. If you had just picked up the pen and signed, like some men of the cloth I have met would have done, you would have had your five million, but I would have gone away disappointed that a toddler with downy cheeks had declared war on the principalities and powers. Your reward for checking out my *bona fides* is another five million. *If* I check out, and *if* you sign, there will be ten million at your fingertips."

"What do you think I might spend it on? Just curious." Tom's stomach was churning like a cement mixer with one brick in it.

"You know. Attorneys. Newspaper ads. Purchased air time. Private detectives. Security details. These guys are gonna fight *dirty*. They will know the rules much better than you do, and they will ignore every mother's son of them." He stopped for a moment, and then smiled, "And, of course, you can pay yourself back out of this fund for whatever it will cost you to check me out."

"All right, then," Tom said. "Before seeing you off, since I have you right here, let me begin checking you out now. If you wouldn't find that offensive?"

Trip chuckled again. "Not at all. Appreciate it."

"So tell me about yourself," Tom started in. "Were you born and raised in Alaska . . .?" And so they just talked for twenty minutes or so, with Tom asking the kind of questions he was accustomed to ask when interviewing prospective candidates for teaching positions. He was certainly expecting different kinds of answers, which he certainly got, but he thought that all the same questions would do. They had just gotten to establishment of the foundation, the reasons for it, and the story behind it, when Maria buzzed through. "Your eleven o'clock is here."

"Thank you, Maria. Just a few more minutes."

Tom turned back to Trip. "Back to the purpose of your visit? Maybe you are overstating things just a little—?"

"Not a bit of it, friend. How many friends of the college do you have on your board—you know, the ones who will need to have your back?"

"Ten, including the chairman. And four already don't have my back."

"Ah. How many of them could survive an *honest* IRS audit? And how many would buckle under the threat of a dishonest one?"

Tom swallowed, saying nothing. He thought, involuntarily and somewhat guiltily, about one of them, whose heart he *personally* believed to be about as black as his grandfather's leather Bible, which was pretty black.

"And are all of them true-blue straight arrows, faithful to their wives in the ways intended by the standard marriage vows? No motel porn? No possibility of tawdry histories in their Internet browsers? No sexy Waffle House waitresses?"

Tom's expression revealed more to Trip than he wanted it to. He didn't know anything definite about the personal lives of about five of his board members. The ones he knew about he just assumed were decent men, although he had suspicions here and there, and so he was naturally a little bit nervous about what might happen if the bad guys started turning over flat rocks in the garden in their search for little black beetles.

"And most of them are pastors, right? Men who are used to having their way in their little Southern fiefdoms? Men who haven't ever been in a fight over anything more important than which way the yellow lines in the new parking lot were going to go? If I am the bad guys over on the other side, I am doing opposition research on *all* of those stooges, even as we speak. No, ten million should do it."

"For someone not sure about God and the church, you seem to have an awareness of how things sometimes go."

Trip winced. "I have had three pastors in my life. The first two ran off with somebody else's wife. The third one ran off with mine."

Tom sat up startled, and started to look around in his head for something to say.

"No, no—no need." Trip held up his right hand, as though he were about to take an oath. "On the Sundays I believe in God, which is usually in the summer—I suspect myself partly because theology shouldn't be based on something like the sun being up—I watch church on the television and mutter to myself. The one doctrine I have never had any trouble with is the one about sin. I know all about that one, even in the winter, my own included."

With that he looked intently at Tom. "I already know *you* have a backbone. But I also know this is a team sport, and that you will have some weak spots in your line. If your left tackle is a weenie, they are going to find that out right away, and run their plays there all night long. If *your* backbone is going to be any help to those nameless others, you are going to need a checkbook. Here's my card, here's the checkbook, and here is the paper you would have to sign and send in.

Do all the checking on me and my foundation you need to, and drop me a note when I clear. I can tell you right now there is no fruity stuff, but you need to find that out yourself. If there *were* fruity stuff, I wouldn't know about it. And you have somebody waiting on you."

They both stood up and shook hands. Tom wondered briefly why his backbone didn't always feel as strong as it apparently looked to people like Trip. Did he know more than they did, or did they know more than he did? He gave up after a few seconds, and they walked out into the front office. Maria stood up and came out from behind her desk, and started to walk Mr. Akroyd to the elevator. "No need, missy," he said, "though I appreciate it greatly. I know I walk like I have a bad case of the old age creaks, but it is actually because of a barrel that fell on my foot from an unconscionable height, giving me about three times as many bones in my left foot as I had there before. But I am not as old as I walk."

Maria was naturally geared to move in empathetic directions whenever she could. "Oh! I am so sorry about your foot . . ."

Trip laughed, waved her off, thanking her again. "No, no," he said. "I really needed to get out of the field, and had postponed that move about five years later than I should have. This made it necessary for me to sit by my fire every day." He winked at Dr. Tom, who had already welcomed his next customer, and had turned back at his door to wave farewell to his benefactor. The wink was much as to say that he thanked God for the accident, at least on those days when he believed in God.

7. NEW YORK EXCEPTIONALISM

THE TRIP WAS UNEVENTFUL. TOM, MARIA, AND three student staffers from CVBC had flown up to New York so that Tom could be interviewed by Willow Sloane, a well-known personality with CNN. The staffer interns were not really necessary, but were the result of some travel policies that had been established by the board as the result of an unfortunate indiscretion on the part of the president of the college some twenty-five years prior. As interns, they chaperoned mostly by being underfoot. As students, they mostly just got caught up on their reading.

When the invitation for the interview came, there had been much discussion about whether to do it or not, but Don Carpenter's counsels had prevailed.

"Tom, you are quick on your feet. You are winsome, and we need for people to see winsome. From what most of them are reading, you have fangs that drip blood, and that is not the same as dripping winsomeness. We need for them to see you smile and have themselves a little cognitive dissonance. If we try to ride things out the way we have been doing, they will just use you as a punching bag until the stuffing is all over the floor of the gym."

If Trip Akroyd had been there, he would have added that Tom would *need* to be quick on his feet because if he, Akroyd, knew his onions, this had all the markings of a booby-trap interview. And it did, too.

So the flight to New York had been placid and boring, the way Tom liked his flights. He had never been to the big town before—and they went there a full day before the morning segment with Willow Sloane. Because they were going to be in New York, it had been an easy thing to schedule two other interviews in addition and fly up a day early. One was for satellite radio and the other was with Fox.

Dr. Tom was affected by the spectacle of this throbbing mound of concrete, but not bedazzled. He spent the day going from skyscraper to skyscraper, each one with an impressive security entrance on the ground floor. He kept getting the feeling that once you got past those security checkpoints, you could have your run of the whole country, digitally speaking. And in every last one of those buildings, there were women in striking outfits walking through those offices and hallways apparently like so many tasty treats—red M&Ms in a skyscraper full of trail mix. So to speak.

That first day of interviews had gone well, although the one with Fox had been (surprisingly, to Tom) the bumpiest. That interview had been conducted by one Garrety Monroe, who was, as best Tom could tell, an incarnate set of talking points from the Republican National Committee. He was genuinely nice off-camera, but as soon as they were rolling he turned into something else, something simultaneously unctuous and hard-edged. There had apparently been plenty of oil left over after he fixed his hair, and so he had figured out a way to work that into his smile.

"Dr. Collins, I think that a lot of freedom-loving Americans are missing your point. You are a conservative Bible college president, and so lots of folks out there *want* to support you. The values you teach are heartland values. We want our young people to learn these heartland values . . . but I think that *they* think that you are trying to insult our flag somehow, and our exceptional way of life. So, speaking of that word, how does this troubling action of yours fit with American exceptionalism?"

"Well, I am not sure that it really does, Garrety."

"Excuse me? Are you sure you want to say that?

"Well, yes. I do believe in a certain *form* of American exceptionalism. James Madison and the others wrote a Constitution that clearly didn't trust Americans at all. That

really was exceptional. But now that we have started to believe in our own uniqueness . . . well, that's not exceptional at
all. Everybody has done that, from the Babylonians on down."

"But I don't see why you feel it is necessary to dishonor
our flag like this. Because when you dishonor our flag, you
dishonor those who have fought under it, our brave men and
women in uniform—"

"Garrety, I don't dishonor the flag at all. What we are doing at Choctaw Valley is a form of subordinated *honor*, not
dishonor at all. Burning the flag, or desecrating it in other
ways—that would be dishonor. If I were doing that, a lot of
the people yelling for my head now would be defending me.
But subordinating the flag to *God*? How is that a dishonor-
able place to be? Even the Pledge says *under* God."

"But Dr. Collins, you don't have a God flag up there. You
have a Christian flag there. Why can't you put up a flag to a
generic god? One that would include all people of faith?"

"Well, people might mistake that for a white surrender
flag," Dr. Tom chuckled.

"Yes, but seriously? Wouldn't that be better?"

"But we couldn't do that. We are a Christian college. We
don't worship a generic god. The world wasn't created by a
generic god. A generic god did not send His Son to die for us.
And that is because a generic god doesn't exist."

Garrety had no talking points for this one, and without
them, he was almost entirely marooned. And on the question

of whether a nonexistent god could have created the world, he felt like he had suddenly gotten out of his depth, theologically speaking. So he went back to his point about exceptionalism, something he could talk about all day long, and where he felt a bit more secure. He hadn't understood the point that Dr. Tom was making about it earlier, so he still thought he was safe.

"Why don't you believe in American exceptionalism, Dr. Collins?"

"Well, as I mentioned, there is a form of it that I actually do believe in. The Founders were remarkable in their foresighted ability to construct a form of government that distrusted all future generations of American politicians so thoroughly. They knew we were just one more nation. *That* was exceptional." Dr. Tom could hear the music for the break coming up, so he hastened to finish his point. "So the fact remains that the Founders did not trust Americans. And from what I have seen the last few weeks, I can't say as I blame them."

>>>X<<<

But the second morning in New York was the main reason they had come up. Willow Sloane's program—interestingly named *Touch & Go*—had over ten million viewers regularly, and Don had thought an appearance there would be really strategic. Tom was up early that morning, and was going through some notes he had jotted down on the plane, organizing them.

It was still pretty early, but he was going to have to head over to the studio in about fifteen minutes—he was going to meet Maria and their staffers in the lobby. CNN had a limo coming for them. While he was rearranging and composing his thoughts, the phone jangled suddenly. Six thirty? Who could that be? He picked it up. "Tom speaking."

A female voice on the other end of the line started speaking rapidly and quietly, without identifying herself. Tom could scarcely make out what she was saying. She was speaking breathlessly, like she was afraid of being walked in on and caught, which she was.

"Excuse me? Could you speak up?" Tom asked.

"Yes. I'll try. Listen carefully. I am a believer, and my grandma went to Choctaw Valley. I work here at CNN, and nobody here knows I am a believer. Only been here three months. Listen. The interview this morning is an ambush. They told you that they wanted to talk to you about the flag . . . and it is possible they might get to that. But they are going to lead off with trying to blame you for that Dearborn riot, and then they are going to ask you about when you first slept with your late wife."

"What?"

"So you either need to be ready for questions like that, or be a no-show. I wouldn't recommend the no-show option though. They know how to make hay out of that kind of thing. Especially since you flew up here for the interview."

"Look . . . sorry, don't know your name. Thanks very much. *Thank* you."

On the way over to the studio, Maria and the others thought Tom was being unusually quiet, but inside his head, it was a total racket. He was thinking furiously, cooking up appropriate responses, and banging around all kinds of pots and pans in the process. Dearborn, Dearborn, Darla, Darla. Tom had never been so thankful for a twenty-minute warning in his life.

In the foyer of the studio, they were greeted by an executive producer named George Somebody, and then Willow herself came out a minute later. She was tall, and striking, and commanding, and had thick auburn hair down to her shoulders. When introduced, Maria and Willow circled each other warily, but without the circling.

Willow smiled widely, and shook Maria's hand. "Very good to meet you." *How can someone that gorgeous not be in television? Is this a trick?*

Maria returned the smile, but said nothing. *How can someone that beautiful be so . . . not? I'm just curious.*

Tom was escorted into the studio to be wired up, and to get his makeup, and the others were shown into a small room behind glass where they could see and hear everything. The minutes flew by. When their segment was due to start, Willow did the setup flawlessly, and then they went into a two-min-ute video background piece on the whole controversy.

"Well, there you have it," Willow said, when the attention of America was back on her, where it belonged. "And here this morning, we have the person at the center of this very *odd* controversy—Dr. Tom Collins. Welcome, Dr. Collins."

"Thanks for having me." *All right so far.*

"Look, before we get to the flag issue proper, I wanted to ask you a couple of related questions."

"All right." *Incoming!*

"I trust you have been following the news, and so you should know all about the riot in Dearborn two days ago. I was particularly interested in the interview done with that young Michigan lad named Abdul. His haunting story has captured the attention of Americans everywhere, particu-larly as he explained how it made him feel to hear his be-loved Pledge to the American flag recited with the name of *Christ* inserted as it was. So my question is this—do you in the fundamentalist community take *any* responsibility for the damage that has been done in Dearborn, not to mention the damage done to our national unity?"

Dr. Tom closed his eyes briefly, a slow blink, and thanked God for sending Trevor Smith into his life. "Well, I would say two things, Willow. Well-informed news outlets have known about this for some days, and have been reporting on it, but the first thing is that if your viewers go to the Choctaw Valley Bible

College website, they can see a video clip of the person who was responsible for inserting the name of *Christ* into the Pledge. And he was a gentleman whose only association with us was adversarial. So if a 'community' needs to take responsibility here for the Dearborn mess, it would be the journalistic community."

Well-informed news outlets? Journalistic community? All right, Dr. Tom-man. Just for that, my next question is going to be high and inside.

"But let me continue," Tom said. "Suppose we *had* done that. We didn't do it, but supposing we had. Why should anybody riot over something like that?"

"Well, because their deepest religious sensibilities were offended—"

Tom shook his head. "Don't you remember when the Southern Baptists rioted in Birmingham over that Piss Christ exhibit?"

Willow Sloane shook her head.

"Well, don't you at least remember the three days of rioting when the Catholics burned down three city blocks in Pittsburgh over that painting of the Virgin Mary done with elephant dung?"

Willow fell for it completely. "No, I don't remember that."

"Me neither," Dr. Tom said.

They both just sat there for a second. A half-second later Willow flushed a noticeable red, visible to those viewers who had HD, and moved to her next question, livid.

As they had been digging up their dirt on Tom, the research department had been told, by a now radico-lesbian who had been an old roommate of Tom's deceased wife, that Tom and Darla had slept together twice during their engagement. She had been very earnest, and told her story with eyes that were wide and very round.

"Is it true," Willow began, "that you and your wife had sex together before you were married?" *High and inside, nothing. She was aiming for his helmet.*

Inside the booth, Maria jumped up, her eyes on fire. She started moving for the door, then thought better of it. She came back and sat down on her stool like a pile driver.

"No, that's not true." Tom said.

"That's all you're going to say?" Willow asked, leaning forward in her toughest interview posture, the one she had used on Senator Pullan when he still thought it was possible to save his career. *That* interview.

"That's all I *need* to say. But I will give you a couple of additional comments, if you like. It is not true. But in the spirit of 1 Corinthians 7:9, it would have been completely true if we hadn't moved the wedding date up to *keep* it from being true. There were some close calls. Next, I think I know the only possible source of your information. If I were you, I would expend a little more time with due diligence in that department. The last time I talked to your source, she was saying that *any* kind of cancer could be prevented with an ointment made out of orange juice concentrate and locally-sourced barbecue sauce. She would probably sell you a bottle if you asked."

It wasn't until that moment that Tom decided to take the offensive. But things seemed to be rolling, so he just kept rolling.

"And last, since this kind of background history is apparently an important qualification for those who must answer questions on your show, at the very least it would seem the same qualification would apply to those who are privileged to ask such questions. So would you mind if I asked you a question in the same vein?"

At this, Willow jumped like someone had punched a sharp awl through the seat of her chair, and almost went over backwards. The sharp toe of her right shoe clicked on the coffee table in front of them, and the coffee cup went over, although it was nearly empty. And at that very moment, Dr. Tom became the darling of the conservative movement, flag or no flag. Apparently, their love for the red, white and blue, great though it was, was overshadowed by their general detestation of Willow Sloane. The interrelationships of political symbols is a subject that is sometimes hard to understand.

In the booth, Maria had jumped out of her seat again, but for a completely different reason than Willow had. She was thrilled beyond description, and had the Italian hand gyrations to go with it.

Tom had been ready with a follow-up question to ask because—always a fast reader—when the interview had first been set up, he had gone down to the nearest big box book monster store and bought Willow Sloane's autobiography, *Free to Say*. Dr. Tom had been counseling students and faculty members for years, and there were some lines in that book that were actually not that hard to read between.

The producer, thinking fast, cut to a commercial. Willow stood up, wheeled on him, and snapped, "Get the next guest ready . . . we are done with this segment."

"Got it," he said. "The developer of the power diet, coming up."

Willow Sloane spun back around, and pointed a trembling finger at Tom. "And I will not say goodbye to you. How *dare* you?"

Tom was already standing up, and wending his microphone cord back out of his shirt. "I like that," he said. "How dare *I*?"

"Yes, how dare you?"

"You asked me that question without warning. I did not ask you that question. I asked you *if* I could, like a gentleman. Furthermore, the name of your position is *host*. My office is that of *guest*. You should have been more prepared, and I am sorry it didn't work out for you."

She turned away abruptly, fuming. "Get out," she said.

Dr. Tom had gotten the microphone out of his shirt by this time, and had also recovered the little fuzzy cap that went on the end of it, gave the bundle of wires to the engineer, and stepped off the little platform.

"We should at least work on being pleasant," Tom said, as he moved away. "My understanding is that we will both be at your publisher's cocktail party tonight, isn't that right? Well, good day."

Willow's shoulders froze. She had forgotten completely about that. He was going to be there, and she had to be there. Her publicist had insisted on it. She had to be present, no option. Her next book deal depended on it. And *he* was going to be there. That had seemed like a good idea at the time, cadging him an invitation for an event he would have to attend, after having been humiliated on national television. Now it was looking like *he* was going to be fine. She was furious, and badly rattled. As soon as she got off this damn set, she was going to go get herself a drink.

Dr. Tom, followed by the others, was headed for the exit, down a long hallway. At the end of the hallway, by the last doorway, a cute, wholesome looking girl was standing, alone, by the right side of the door. She had a silver cross necklace on, and looked straight at Tom as he was passing by, smiled and winked. Tom nodded cordially, without slowing down.

Maria, just behind him, saw the whole thing, but placed an entirely different construction on it. She was very upset at the *impudence* of girls these days, for about ten minutes. When they got back out to the limo, Tom told them all about his early morning phone call, and how they all owed a great debt of gratitude to Aubrey, as her name, judging from her name tag, apparently was. Maria decided to forgive her for winking at Tom. Mostly.

》》X《《

After the Willow Sloane triumph, the only remaining talk radio interview that afternoon was almost too easy. Anything would be an anticlimax after making Willow jump a foot and a half, but Tom was still on a roll, and was prepared to have a bit of fun. Now that he had tried taking the offensive—now that he had tasted journalistic blood—he wasn't sure he could ever go back. The host, Brent Sewell, was a hard leftist, made no bones about it, and tried to recover the ground that he instinctively knew had been lost by Willow. Something had to be done that would generate more media buzz than "the Willow Sloan jump" looked like it was going to.

Consequently, the cash value of Tom's exchange with him all happened in the first ten minutes, and wound up being played repeatedly on conservative talk radio for two weeks afterward. Tom was in the zone. He was like a basketball player who looks at the hoop and sees only a metal circle with a twenty-foot diameter. Looking back, he didn't know how he'd managed to sit through all those board meetings without saying anything more than "does anyone second the motion to approve the minutes."

After the introductions, and whatnot, Brent went straight for the throat. "So, Dr. Tom, I wanted to ask you about reports child pornography has been discovered on your computer."

"Reports?"

"Yes, reports." This was actually based on a couple of politicized and very randy gossip sites, which had Brent had read carelessly, which compounded the problem of the posts having been written carelessly. "I understand that some anonymous hackers say that they got into your computer, and found the mother lode of child porn. How are you going to handle this next layer of controversy."

Dr. Tom laughed. "By laughing at it. It is not another layer of controversy at all."

"Sure, try to laugh it off. There are people out there who are going to need some answers."

"Okay, then, here it is," Tom said. "Let's pretend that this even happened, which it probably didn't. Let's just work with the story that *you* say happened. Pretend you just told me that you read about some people who crept into my house in the middle of the night and they swear they found some porn in my library or under my bed. And you want to maintain that they are dishonest enough to break into my house like this, but honest enough not to *plant* the porn there? How did you get criminals like this with just the right balance of honesty and dishonesty?"

Brent paled, and realized that he was not going to be the darling of all those who wanted this situation cleaned up. At least not this time. He drifted, without enthusiasm, back toward a standard interview.

Out in the waiting room, listening to the interview, Maria was so proud of Tom she thought she might cry.

>>>X<<<

The ceiling of the room where the cocktail party was held was thickly covered with numerous chandeliers, the hotel ballroom kind of chandelier, and with all of them putting out the kind of light you might see at the lower wattage end of a brown out. The lights, however, were not flickering, which made you realize that somebody was doing it all on purpose.

Despite the lighting, or perhaps because of it, the room was filled with major media figures, television personalities, editors and other detritus from the publishing world, a handful of decrepit rock stars, and throbbing electropop. *Oom cha oom cha oom cha*. Oh, and money. The room was full of money in very adult amounts, Manhattan scale, while the crackling envy and flirtation levels were all still stuck in junior high, Hoboken scale.

The "atrocious lighting," as Dr. Tom summed it up, made it look like one of Dante's circles done up in sepia tones. "That's the first thing about all this that I would like to point out." Maria smiled at him. "Here is the second thing. How long are we expected to be at this monstrosity?" Tom asked Maria. This was about forty-five seconds after they entered.

"I believe that an hour on the premises would satisfy all debts of honor," she replied. "I told the woman at CNN that you had a flight out first thing, and that we couldn't tarry here. I honestly don't know why she was so keen on us coming. But she was."

"Okay, so we are here because the booking lady at CNN wanted us to be here. What is everybody *else* doing here? What is this thing *for*?"

Maria shook her head. "I don't honestly don't know what the excuse is. My guess is the celebration of some kind of award. They give each other awards all the time. But the actual function is what I believe they call networking." As she shook her head in reply, her raven hair moved back and forth sinuously, and Tom didn't think he noticed it. *Probably didn't,* he thought. *Better not,* he thought again.

Tom cleared his throat in his best imitation of his grandfather, who had decided and very pointed opinions about how our nation was circling the cultural drain, and who, whenever he would watch the evening news, would clear his throat in just that same way, and say, "It ain't the way it used to be, I'll tell you that." He was the original church curmudgeon. Tom could do a passable imitation whenever he wanted.

After about half an hour, halfway done, Maria left for a few moments and came back from the bar with a refill of her Coke, as they helpfully called *every* soft drink back home. And when she got back to where Tom was she noticed—as it would have been impossible not to—that Willow had arrived, and was ensconced next to Dr. Tom, six inches away from his left elbow. That woman's anger from the incident of that morning had apparently evaporated, which Maria knew most certainly could *not* be the case, but she was acting like everything was all fine, anyway. Maria could see at a glance that Willow must have settled in on some peculiar kind of feminasty revenge, and that she needed to be near Tom to do it. Her outfit was like a sale at Macy's—forty percent off—and Maria started to fume, but then checked herself. *No need, no need.*

Maria gracefully joined the chatting circle on the other side of it, holding her drink a bit more tightly than she usually would. She noticed that she was doing that, and made herself relax. *No need.* She exhaled gracefully, and then a moment later did it again. Nobody had as of yet introduced a topic, so they were all still talking about weather and other oddments from the day's news. What was she going to do about this little bit of tacky business across the way? Whatever Willow was going to pull, Tom was sure to be unsuspecting and defenseless.

But suddenly, unsought, a cloud of serenity descended on Maria and she quietly settled into her mission. *This is what I was made for,* she thought. She had always felt bad about the effect she usually had on other women, and she had never been able to figure out what on earth she could do about ameliorating that effect. Whenever she tried anything, it always just made things worse. But here . . . here was an opportunity to go clear in the other direction and have whatever effect she might have with a clean conscience. *Bombs away.*

So she just waited for a moment until she caught Willow's eye, which given the competitive circumstances wasn't that hard, and made sure her eyes were filled with sympathy. She parted her lips slightly, revealing her very white teeth, and quickly ran her tongue across them. Willow reacted appropriately, but ever so slightly, closed her mouth, and excused herself. She clearly needed to go to the ladies room to see if she had gotten lipstick on her teeth. She hadn't, but as she left, Maria gracefully glided into the place where Willow had been standing.

When Willow came back, her frustration was invisible to everyone but Maria. Willow took her place across the way, where Maria had been standing just few moments before, but the cloud of serenity that Maria had been standing in was apparently not there anymore. The chatter went on, as though nothing were happening under the surface. But there was a great *deal* happening under the surface. If that conversation had been the North Atlantic just several generations back, there would have been U-boats everywhere.

Maria suddenly felt a tap on her shoulder. It was Ronny, one of the students who had been sent to the Big Apple with them. He needed to speak with her outside for a moment. Maria reluctantly relinquished her place next to Tom, and

walked out with Ronny, who had (as it turns out) a completely trivial and unnecessary question to ask her. He actually had desperately needed an excuse of some kind to get
an insider's glimpse of that Manhattan party—for he fully intended to go back to his grandfather in Mississippi with tales
from Babylon. His grandfather was a revival preacher named
Stump Hutchins from the Tupelo old school, and was capa-
ble, whenever he got going good, of preaching a pretty wide
swath of blue ruin. This little snapshot from Sodom was most
certainly going make an appearance in future sermons—the
tinkling glasses full of AHL-ko-hawl being featured not least
on the litany of abuses.

All this was going to make for some very good sermon fod-
der, but Maria failed to grasp the blessing that this future edifi-
cation would bring to those listening saints down in Mississippi.
They didn't enter into it at the moment. She swallowed down
her annoyance, answered Ronny's question, counted to three
by the door and then poked her head back in again.

Sure enough, Willow was right next to Dr. Tom again,
doing her level best to fall out of her dress. She was going
to step on her bust line in a minute if she wasn't more careful. Maria quietly stepped back out into the hallway that
led from the ballroom down to the foyer of the hotel. She
walked briskly down that hall and out to the concierge,
and asked if the bar in the ballroom had a phone. It did,
as it turns out, and so the concierge helpfully handed that

number over, trying not to stammer as he talked with her. Later that night, talking to his roommate, he spent forty-five minutes describing Maria, which his roommate enjoyed for the first ten minutes or so. But oblivious to most of *that* fairly subdued drama, Maria headed back to the ballroom, entering the number as she went. When she was just outside the ballroom, she hit call, and waited a moment for the bartender to pick up.

"Yes, hello. I am very sorry—I know this is unusual, but would it be possible to speak with Willow Sloane? I understand that she is there." Maria did not add that it was an emergency, for reasons having to do with the ninth commandment, but her voice sounded pretty serious. And *perhaps* urgent. *Maybe* it was an emergency.

It *was* highly unusual, and would have gone nowhere if the barkeep had not been eager for an opportunity to speak with Willow Sloane himself, however briefly. He said, "Hold on," laid the receiver on the bar, and walked across the way to where Tom's group was standing. "Excuse me," he said, catching Willow's eye, "there is a phone call for you at the bar. Sounded like an emergency," he said. "Wouldn't bother you otherwise," he added helpfully.

About halfway to the bar, Willow had a feeling of sudden misgiving, and stopped. She wheeled around to see Maria standing right next to Tom, with an look on her face that was expressive of absolutely nothing. Willow swore to herself, and

walked in a sort of high heel stiletto stomp over to the bar—
too late now—in order to verify that she had been scammed.
She picked up the receiver, caught about a second of the dial
tone, and threw it down in exasperation. The bar keep, who
had been looking forward to a bit more conversation than
that, was disappointed.

By the time Willow got back to the group, it was apparent
to more of them than just Maria that all was not well with
her. She was exasperated and, like many in her position, did
not wear her exasperation well. Her intention to be standing
where Maria was now standing was evident to some of the
group, and while she was not yet at the point where she might
throw an elbow, it was clear she was thinking about it.

Maria, meantime, was still standing in her serenity cloud,
which was moving around with her. She had found her
groove, and knew that she was walking in the good works
that God had prepared in advance for her to do. *Blessed be
the Lord my strength, which teacheth my hands to war, and
my fingernails, which are a classy crimson, to fight.* (For the
Barancho family, fingernail polish, and things like it, were
the only area where fundamentalism had lost to the Italian
heritage argument.) She was tempted to smile, but fought it
down. This was deadly serious, and she did not want to appear to be taunting. *Rejoice not when thine enemy falleth, lest
the Lord see it, and He turn away His wrath.* She shook her
head at the temptation, and her earrings flashed.

Tom, meanwhile, appeared to be among the oblivious. There was high drama going on to his west and northwest, but he was engaged in earnest conversation to the northeast. When he had learned that they were to stay there an hour, he had accepted his fate like a man of courage, and decided simply to chat people up for the duration of his sentence. He was currently engaged in a quasi-political discussion with a producer of some news thing from NPR. Nobody had brought up the flag issue, politely enough, and so they were spending their time working on their issues through proxies. He knew that Maria would give him the high sign when he was free to go.

Willow had a dangerous glint in her eye. "Maria, dear, would you mind if Jonathan here took a picture of Tom and me together? We neglected to do that this morning, and we really should have something for the website . . ." At that moment Maria fortunately saw Ronny circling around behind her to ask another entirely superfluous question. Babylon apparently required more research.

Maria said, "Certainly, certainly," and reached out to take Willow's hand, turning her around to take her place, facing Jonathan, he who had the camera. He was some functionary or other who was accompanying Willow, and she had impressed his service with the camera on his phone. Maria, meantime, was saying something encouraging and reassuring, along the lines of "Here we go, that's it." But as soon as Willow was facing the right direction, which was away from Maria, she shoved

Tom off to the right just a few steps, and quietly scooped up the greatly astonished Ronny who had just arrived and placed his arm in Willow's, like the father of the bride giving his daughter away. Maria stepped out in front to look at the couple, and acted like all was well. Tom's eyebrows were arched as Maria stepped gracefully away to make room for the flash. *What occureth?,* he seemed to be saying.

Jonathan hadn't really been paying attention to who was who, and had been fussing with the focus on his phone, and so even though he was the only one looking straight at them, he didn't notice the switch. So Willow was standing there with Ronny, looking straight ahead, trying to smile for the camera, which meant that she had to swallow down her grim satisfaction. She was of course thinking she had Tom in her power (several recent cocktails may have helped with this—not to mention the stiff drinks she had poured herself in preparation for the party), and so as Jonathan counted down, three, two . . . she quickly allowed herself something of a wardrobe malfunction. This wasn't too hard because she was almost already a walking wardrobe malfunction, but regardless, *that'll* show him. *He can't put it in his stupid Bible college newsletter, obviously, but everyone else in the country will see it, and he will be a laughingstock.* What the photoshop idiot at Gawker was not able to do, *she* could do. So everything was swell until their mini photo shoot was all done, and she turned and saw Ronny, who had turned a peculiar shade of crimson, and then she saw Tom and Maria standing off to the side. Together.

And at that moment, all pretense was gone, and she exploded into the kind of fury she usually reserved for her office staff whenever something went wrong. She snatched a drink from a passing tray and hurled it in Maria's direction. Unfortunately for her new plan, while her aim was good, she had not counted on a very recent decision made by a Pulitzer Prize-winning poet to walk just in front of Maria on her way to the bar again.

The poet's name, which does not matter *that* much to the narrative, other than to spice it up a bit, was Tingsted Taki-Smith. Her name certainly did not affect the trajectory of the cocktail glass, which bounced off her forehead, sending its contents straight up into the air, with the glass itself heading off at a ninety degree angle, parallel to the floor for a second or so. But then it hit, making a most satisfactory shattering sound, causing all conversation in that region of the party to cease. Everyone wheeled and stared, and in the background the sound track for this unfolding drama was simply *oom cha oom cha oom cha.*

Fortunately for Maria and Tom, who needed to make themselves scarce, and were even now making their preparations to do so, Tingsted Taki-Smith had already been thinking that the party had been inadequately focused on her. There had been a singular lack of notice and appreciation. People had been talking to and about *other* people. Having a cocktail bounced off her forehead provided the necessary opportunity. Any attention is better than no attention. She clutched at her face and began to wail loudly and weave wildly.

After a moment or two of inarticulate keening, she fell to her knees and began to heave sob. This striking performance was certainly having its intended effect. Even Willow was startled out of her furious desire to get at or otherwise maim Maria, and the cold realization began to dawn on her that Tingsted Taki-Smith—of the Cleveland Taki-Smiths—might present some sort of legal difficulties to her and her future career. After all, had she not just banked a cocktail glass off the forehead of the poetess, and had she not thrown it for no apparent reason? Willow had two options—to huff it out of there and brazen the consequences through her lawyer, who wasn't that good, or to gather around the stricken poet with armfuls of solicitude. After weighing her options quickly, she decided that while she definitely had the former as her heart's desire, her wiser self counseled the latter. She rushed forward, and knelt beside the stricken poet. She wanted to be subtle in how she introduced the subject of bookings on her show, but as it turned out, Taki-Smith was not at all concerned about subtlety. As long as the spotlight was pointed the right direction, she was good with it, no matter how transparent the whole thing was.

This poor woman's poetry—which is brought up here only to help us make sense of the larger narrative—was the kind of poetry that focused on how the poet *felt*. True, there is not much here to distinguish it from the vast watery sea of how all the other poets felt, but Taki-Smith had a peculiar genius for it. Her volume of verse that had won the Pulitzer Prize was not titled *The Pale Parabola of Joy*, but it might as well have been.

Maria looked at Dr. Tom, and her manner was all business. "I believe that you have a flight first thing in the morning," she said.

"Yes, I do," he said. He was now, for the very first time that evening, reluctant to go. The behavior of Tingsted Taki-Smith on the floor, who had just now ground her hand heavily into a shard of the shattered cocktail glass, and who was making the most of it, was promising to develop in even more interesting directions. "But," he said, "we should really go." When Willow looked up a few moments later, they were entirely gone.

And, on the up side, as a matter of side interest, while Ronny did have some explaining to do with his grandfather, the revival preacher who thought that anything so soft as rock ribs were characteristic of liberalism, he was *eventually* able to do it. Ronny had to explain it three times, and he had to rededicate his life at the revival meeting and give his testimony about how he was snatched from the very lip of the crater of Hell, but when he was done, everything was quite satisfactory.

Back at the hotel, Tom and Maria walked slowly across
the lobby, which had that glassy and glossy feel that high-
er-end lobbies can have, punctuated with ferns. As they
walked, commenting on the glimpse of New Yorkery that
the cocktail party had provided them, Maria looked across
the lobby and saw Ronny making his way across to them.
He was clearly being more than a little officious, largely because his two forays into the cocktail orgy shortly before
had made him a chaperon in the technical sense only, now
struggling with compensatory issues. He was superfluous,
but was striving to be diligent at it. The other two student
interns were off studying like they were supposed to, and
maybe flirting a little bit. They were frankly glad that Ronny
was gone. But Maria saw Ronny coming, was not so glad,
and was therefore prepared.

"Ronny," she said, as he came up and before he had
a chance to speak, "Dr. Tom is flying out first thing in the
morning. Could you check with the concierge and make sure
that the shuttle will be running by four a.m.? If it is, no worries, but if not, could you have a message sent to Dr. Tom's
room letting him know? That way he will know if he has to
get a cab. Thanks so much," she concluded with the finality
that lets a person know that the conversation, however much
of a delight it had been up to that point, was now concluded.

Ronny nodded, not quite sure how the signal had gotten through to him that his presence was unnecessary and

undesired. But it had gotten through to him, and so he headed off to the main desk.

Two other hotel guests got on the elevator with Tom and Maria. They both got off, almost immediately, on the second or third floor. Tom was staying on the tenth, and Maria on the fourteenth, in accordance with the protocols. As soon as the doors closed behind them, Tom cleared his throat.

"So. I wanted to make sure I thanked you for running interference tonight."

"With Ronny?"

Tom laughed. "Well, that too. You must have been in the groove. You have been running interference all evening . . ."

Maria's eyebrows went up. *Tom noticed things like that?*

Just to be sure, she said, "What do you mean?"

"With Willow Sloane," he said. "She was gunning for me from the moment she got there, and you seemed to have an absolute genius for getting in between. Thanks very much. I really appreciated it."

Maria pursed her lips, very slightly. "You're welcome."

"You know that she was nearly frantic by the end of the evening?"

Maria nodded. "Well, yes, I know about that. She threw a cocktail glass at me. I did notice it."

"Sorry . . . that's not what I meant . . . I meant, do you know *why* she was frantic? You seemed very . . . territorial. You keep people away from me for a living, I know that, and there is no one better at it, I must say, but this seemed quite different somehow . . . not like what you do with pushy curriculum salesmen."

Maria said nothing, but was starting to panic inside. Tom was talking to *her*, and it was personal. Not schedules, not meetings, not appointments. He was talking to *Maria,* about a subject, about *them.* So she said nothing. At least that way she wouldn't say anything wrong.

"You know why she was frantic?" Tom repeated.

Maria was not really sure what to do. They had reached Tom's floor, and he stepped out, looked both ways, still holding the elevator door open. When he looked back in, she finally said, "Well, because she wanted to get close to you and I wouldn't let her."

Tom shook his head. "That was part of it, sure. But the main reason is that the person in between me and her was a lot more beautiful than she was."

Maria swallowed a sudden gasp, like it was a suppressed hiccup. It barely made any noise at all. Her eyes were round, and she simply stood there, just inside the elevator door.

Shoot, thought Tom. *I haven't held back all day, and now I've gone and done it.* Still holding the door, he leaned in and kissed her, holding it for several seconds. "Good night," he said, stepping out and letting go of the door. After the doors closed, Maria walked in tight circles around the ascending elevator, about ten times, holding both hands to her mouth, trying to hold the kiss in place. It must not get away. "Oh, dear, oh, dear, oh, dear," she was saying.

8. CONSEQUENCE AND COINCIDENCE

IN THE MORNING, AFTER A NIGHT FULL OF TOSSING, turning, and *oh dearing*, Maria got up, showered, and got herself dressed and ready for the trip home. She was flying out of LaGuardia at ten a.m. with Ronny and the other student staffers and heading straight home. Dr. Tom had flown out of JFK at seven, and had another two days of travel in front of him before getting back to the college. He needed to meet with several major donors from the past who had suddenly expressed interest in resuming their support. Maria should know. Maria had done all the booking. Maria had been the one who had sent him flying off in the wrong direction. *No one to blame but myself,* she said.

She found herself spending the time alternating between thinking about the kiss and thinking about the fact that he had said she was more beautiful than Willow. And Willow was gorgeous, mostly. She had a hard brittle edge to her beauty that Maria had noticed right off, but that was the kind of thing that women never trusted men to notice. And Tom had noticed. And then he *said* something about it. And then he had kissed her. And so she thought about that for a little while.

As she was letting her hair dry a little before curling it, she sat down at her laptop on the desk, and opened her email. At the very top of her inbox was an email from drtom@cvbc.edu. The time stamp was from five that morning. *Oh, dear, oh, dear* she started and then shook herself. *Stop it,* she said.

Then she spent about five minutes deciding to open it. She knew she was going to open it, that was certainly inevitable. So what was she waiting for?

Not yet, she thought.

It will be better later, how? So she clicked it.

"Dear Maria," he began.

At least it is not "Dear Miss Barancho." That would be bad. This is okay.

> It will have not escaped your notice that I kissed you last night.

In spite of her screaming fantods, Maria laughed out loud. *He was so funny.*

> We obviously need to talk, but because I acted im-
> pulsively, I failed to take into account the fact that I

> was leaving first thing and won't be back to Choctaw
> Valley for a couple of days. We will have to talk then.
> And my apologies.

Talk? Apologies? What was he apologizing for? For kissing her? Or for kissing her *impulsively*? Instead of the way he had planned? Had there been a plan, but then he abandoned it? Or was he apologizing for forgetting he had a flight and kissing her anyway? Did I kiss him back? I think so, but would *he* think that I did? And if he noticed, what would he think of *that*?

And thus the stage was set for Maria to go through several days of dark anguish and exquisite joy, alternating back and forth like a small reciprocating two-cycle engine. This was not the effect Tom had intended. He thought he had declared himself fully—no room for ambiguity. But in her modesty Maria had found room for ambiguity.

〉〉〉✕〈〈〈

At the very same moment that Maria was reading Dr. Tom's emailed sentiments, Gov. Fawgee Prater was also kissing his secretary. It must be said, however, that their shared moment did not exude the same aura of sweet innocence that Tom and Maria's did. It was a study in contrasts.

"Okay, back to business," he said after a moment.

"Back to your *other* business," she replied. Her name, for those keeping track of such things, was Susan. This was a nice balance to the name Fawgee, but since nobody ever saw them together publicly, it was a balance that no one was really in a position to appreciate. Fawgee's wife was named Helen, and this contrast had a similar balancing effect. His first wife had been named Daisy Mae, no kidding, which had been part of the problem in their marriage. As soon as Fawgee had developed his political aspirations, which was pretty soon, he realized that "Fawgee and Daisy Mae" would immediately be forever tagged as the couple from Dogpatch. And even though their state had quite a few Dogpatches, from which a few votes could be squeezed, there wouldn't be enough votes from them to recoup the corresponding losses in the urban areas. He could always change *his* name, but his mother was still alive at that point, and she was a force to be reckoned with. So he had moved on to Helen, who had a normal sounding name.

After that he moved on to Susan, at least off budget. And if his presidential aspirations were ever realized, he had assured Susan that she was the one who would be his First Lady. She was not stupid, but went along with him anyway. If she ever married him, she knew, she would actually be the Third Lady, with other intermediates here and there. She stayed where she was, not because she believed him, but rather because she saw some possible opportunities herself.

Governor Fawgee Prater was the kind of politician who was telegenic enough, but who, if you got closer than ten yards or so, was revealed to be as unctuous and oily as they come. A full crankcase had nothing on him. All the oil was necessary because without it all the moving parts of his personal ambition would burst into flame and melt down into a useless pile of metal.

He nodded at Susan. "Get Parkson on the horn for me," he said.

"Right away," she said, and headed back to her desk.

As he waited for Susan to make the call, Fawgee Prater stood looking out the window of his office, staring coldly at the lit skyline, and flicking the little metal end of his bolo tie. He always wore a bolo tie, thinking it made him more authentic and regional, and as far as the latter characteristic was concerned, it somehow worked, even though it was the wrong region. The same thing went for his cowboy boots— Texas was still a long day's drive west. But the boots enabled one journalistic observer to summarize Prater for his amused colleagues in a superb phrase—he was an ego in boots.

His eyes would glint whenever he wanted something, and he always wanted something. At this moment what he was wanting was Parkson, his chief of staff.

Susan buzzed him, back to being the soul of professionalism. "Parker Parkson on line one," she said.

The governor punched the button and picked up. "Yeah?" he said, somewhat belligerently.

"You called?" Parker said, pleasantly enough.

"Yeah," the governor said. "You still downtown here?"

"Yes, sir."

"Well, then, c'mere." With that the governor dropped the phone back into its base. His chief of staff was in the same office complex, but it was down the hall a ways. It would be a few minutes. Prater walked back to the window and started flicking his bolo tie again. He had flicked it several hundred times when the tap came on his door and Parker Parkson walked in.

He was the kind of operative who exuded competence. He didn't look hard and sneaky, which is why he was so good at being both. He walked over to the nearest chair and sat down in it in a manner that showed that he was far enough into Prater's council that he did not need to behave like an underling. That, and the fact that he knew where all the bodies were buried.

"What's on your mind, boss?" he said.

"This flag thing remains a big deal," the governor said.

"I know—it is huge."

"*I* know it is huge," the governor repeated. "But *you* tell me why it is huge."

Parker nodded. "All right. If we stay on schedule, which we should do, you are declaring your candidacy for president a month from now. If this thing is still boiling, you will be the candidate from the state that has some loon flying the Christian flag above the American flag, for all the world to see. Laughingstock. Pure gold for editorial cartoonists. The *Late*

Show. You are the presumptive front-runner, but there are at least three primary challengers who are in play. Whatever hay they might make out of this remains to be seen, but the incumbent Democrat will surely tag you as someone who is secretly supportive of this Collins guy. However much you denounce it all, he is still flying that thing in your state, and you haven't done anything about it. That good enough?"

"So why can't we just have this Collins guy arrested? For disturbing something or other?"

"Because of Willow Sloane. Collins has managed to befuddle rank and file conservatives and become their darling at the same time. The video clip of her kicking the table during the interview has been viewed online about three million times."

"And we can't let it all go because . . . ?"

"Because his position will be draped around your neck. Where we don't think it belongs."

The governor lurched in another direction. "So tell me again what happened with this board of his. Tell me why it will be better next time. Tell me why you let me down there."

Parker had reported on this at least three times, but he was grateful for this opportunity. He had a little bit more bad news he needed to break.

"We have the votes to require Collins's resignation. We just needed an opportunity to case them. The two question marks were out of town until right before that meeting of theirs, and so we couldn't get to them in time. But since the meeting, our boys have visited them, and both of them folded, as the expression goes, like a cheap suit."

"So? Get another meeting called, and have them vote this guy down the street."

This is where the breaking bad news came in. Parker cleared his throat. "The chairman of the board is a guy named Kramer. He won't budge. It turns out that another meeting cannot be called for six months unless the chairman agrees to call it, and he flat refuses."

"Dirt?"

"He is as clean as a Dutch oven. We turned up a bunch on the others—which is why they flipped so quickly. But Kramer seems to be an actual Christian—like Collins, by the way. He has been pressured by a couple of the other board members to call another meeting, and he just won't do it. He says they already voted on all that."

"What do their bylaws say would go down if something happened to Kramer? Say he had a little accident."

"The vice-chair is a guy named Jones. Friend of Kramer's, and other than that we don't know much about him. The research team didn't turn up anything one way or the other. He voted for Collins in this last go-round. It would be high-risk, low-promise."

The governor nodded, as though happy that murder might turn out to be unnecessary. "So we need to put the screws to Collins directly. What do we have in the tool box?"

"I have several approaches we could open up. One is that Don Carpenter, Choctaw Valley's fund-raiser guy, is an old classmate. I still see him from time to time at reunions. He is not a realist as you and I are, but I think he understands how it operates. I can have a chat with him. Second, we have some friends at the IRS who have already opened files on the board members who continue to support Collins. Third, with regard to Tom himself, he has no immediate family. He lives quietly by himself. Doesn't even have a dog. He has one sister who is very close to him, though, and I think we have found a couple of handles that we could use on her."

At this, the governor chuckled. "All right," he said. "Standard ops then. Nothing traceable. Complete deniability. But however opaque it is to the watching world, it has to be transparent to the folks we are . . . um, influencing. Right?"

"Right. I think I can make all that clear to Don Carpenter. Without saying anything. I will try to connect with him tomorrow."

$$\gg\!\!\times\!\!\ll$$

Dr. Tom arrived back in Choctaw Valley around four in the afternoon. He had time to stop in at the office, but decided not to. He could gather his thoughts from home, get the things he needed, and hit the ground running in the morning. He didn't know it, but this would also give him time that evening to entertain visits from Don Carpenter and Parker Parkson.

He lived on about five acres a couple of miles outside of town. His long, winding driveway went up a long slope between two rows of elms. The house was a modest brick home with a large front lawn. There was a small deck on the side and back, and behind that was a large wooded area, one that looked like it had been planted recently.

Tom clumped up the front walk wearily, unlocked the front door, dropped his briefcase off in his study, went to the fridge for something to drink, settled for fruit juice on ice, and then went back to the study. He fired up his desktop to check his email.

The first email (after one telling him to boost his testosterone, which had inexplicably made it through his spam filter) was one from Kramer. The subject line was "Bad, But Not Unexpected."

"Everyone who voted for you," Kramer wrote, "received a letter from the IRS saying that they are getting audited. They are not playing with nuance or subtlety here. The message is being written in big block letters, and all the gentlemen have managed to read it. They have all contacted me in various ways, and I have disappointed most of them. Several of them told me that they knew you were in the right, but that we couldn't afford this battle. Just thought you should know. Me, I'm sticking to the plan."

Tom was staring at the screen, thinking about Maria, and eating his microwaved dinner when he heard a car driving up. He walked to the front window—his study looked out over the left side of his front lawn—and recognized Don Carpenter's car driving up.

Tom opened the front door, and waited while Don ambled up. "Come in, come in," he said. "Something big must be brewing."

"Sorry to drop in on you like this. Maria said you would likely be back by now, and I thought this was a big enough deal to come out."

"What is it?" Tom escorted Don back to the study.

"I got a letter this morning, registered, saying the college's 501(c)3 status is being reviewed. I knew that the governor had to be behind it and so I emailed an old classmate, Parker Parkson, who is now the governor's chief of staff, to see if I could come visit him. He said that he was actually planning on coming to see me, and that this would save him some gas money. So I drove over there after lunch, and had a heart-to-heart. He didn't say anything overtly, but he let me know in about five different ways that the appearances were not deceiving."

Tom interrupted him. "Did you hear about the board members who voted to keep me?"

Don's eyebrows shot up. "No, what?"

Tom filled him in, reading from Kramer's email. Don sat quietly for a moment. "Look," he said eventually. "Giving is bouncing against the ceiling. This whole thing ought to be a fund-raiser's delight. But these people know where the choke point is. If we lose our tax exemption, all this enthusiasm will be meaningless. People can't write checks if they close the college down. That's what they are going to do. Parkson made that clear enough."

"So what are you recommending, Don?"

"It is no sin to be defeated. You fought a good fight. And I actually do support you. But I think any more would be recklessly unrealistic."

Tom sat quietly. "Well, I have thought about this a great deal. Lots of prayers about it. But no, let's hold on tight."

Don registered disappointment, pretty plainly, and drummed his fingers on the window sill next to him. "Well, Tom," he said, "you are a good man, and a brave one. I don't think this is the wise course of action, though, and I am afraid I am going to have to tender my resignation."

Tom looked alarmed. "Did Parkson threaten you personally?"

Don shook his head. "No, they know I am not a decision-maker. But I honestly don't believe I can do my job in the climate that I think this will generate. I will stay through the end of the month, and Mary Lee can keep the office running while you advertise for a replacement."

Tom walked him to the door, and they shook hands. "Best of luck," they both said.

As he walked back into the house, he heard his one remaining land line ringing in the kitchen. The only one who called him there was his sister Dawn. He picked up, and said, "Hey, sport. I needed to hear from you right now . . ."

His sister interrupted him, distraught, and Tom stopped, like he had walked into a pole. "What? *What* did you say?"

Dawn was normally the most leveledheaded person that Tom would talk to. He had a habit of calling her weekly, even if there was no news to speak of. He would do it just to get a dose of her calm. Not tonight.

She and her husband Frank had not been able to have children, despite wanting them very much. They had tried for years, and then had spent a great deal of time and money working with international adoption agencies. That had finally borne fruit two years ago, with the adoption of two Romanian girls finalized a year later.

"Tom," Dawn said, "We got a letter today from Child Protective Services, saying that they had received several complaints from people in our neighborhood. They want us to come to be interviewed tomorrow, and they want us to bring Kirsten and Kelly in with us to be interviewed separately. They are *clearly* on a fishing expedition . . . and the girls' English is not that great yet. I have heard horror stories about these people, and I don't know what we can do about it!"

Tom immediately thought of the governor. "Did they say anything that would hint that they were motivated by other factors—like this flag situation of mine?"

"Well, yes," Dawn said. "I would have called you about this anyway, but that is part of why I called now. The case worker laughed right before we were done talking, and said that if I had any concerns I could take it up with my brother. It was like they were letting me know what was happening without committing to anything that they couldn't deny . . . oh, Tom . . . if the girls were taken, I don't know if I could bear it . . . we don't have any money for an attorney . . ."

Tom's eye went to the center drawer of his desk, where the checkbook from Trip Akroyd was sitting. Akroyd's *bona fides* had all checked out, just like he had said they would, and some of Tom's friends had not been able to stop talking about what a fine man he was, and how he had saved their bacon at least six times. Tom had signed the paper Trip had left for him, had Maria scan it, and had told her to wait until he told her to send it in. It was seeming to him like that time was upon him.

"Look, Dawn," he said, "I have a way to hire an attorney for you. Consider it done, and I know just the man. I got to know him when I was studying at St. Andrews—he was over there for a year doing some research for a book or something. But he is with the top law firm there in Birmingham. One of the best. We got along great in Scotland, and have exchanged Christmas cards since. I am sure he would help. His name is Melville, John Melville."

"Is he a believer?" Dawn asked.

"Well, he is a Presbyterian. But he is the kind that believes the Bible. And as an attorney, I get the impression he is the kind of lawyer who goes home and sharpens his incisors at night."

"I am thinking that is just what we might want."

"Look, Dawn, I will call you back in the morning. I will be praying like crazy, and I will call you before ten with any news I have. All right, love you. Bye."

As soon as he hung up, Tom sat down and clattered out an email to Maria. "Please send that PDF from Trip Akroyd to that woman at the bank. You have it ready to go, right? If you get this tonight, send it off right away, and call that lady up, whatever her name was, to make sure she got it. I might have to start signing checks pretty soon. Thanks, and I'll talk to you as soon as I can about everything else."

At the very moment he clicked *send*, his doorbell rang. That was odd. It was nine o'clock in the evening. Tom wound his way out of the study, across his living room, and to the front door. He opened it, and was greeted by someone who rang no bells at all, other than the doorbell he had just rung.

"Good evening," Dr. Tom said.

"Evening," the stranger said, extending his hand. "My name is Parker Parkson. I am the governor's chief of staff. I was wondering if you had a moment to talk."

"Sure," Tom said, gesturing. "Come on in. Can I get you anything? Something to drink?"

"No," Parker said. "This shouldn't take long. I just wanted to visit with you briefly."

"Well, then, have a seat," Tom said. They were in the living room, and Parkson sat easily in the chair nearest the door. Tom sat down as well, and said nothing.

"Shall I come straight to the point?"

"Please," Tom said.

Parker spoke very pleasantly, but there was absolutely no give in it. He said, "Dr. Collins, I want you to know that I respect you as an adversary, and to let you know there is nothing personal in any of this."

"Good to know," Tom said.

"Even though I—and the governor, I might add—respect the principled stand you have taken, we are also in a position where we cannot allow this state of affairs to continue. I am sure you understand our perspective."

"Well, I do, actually. Agree to disagree, and all that?"

"No, not exactly," Parker said. "I wanted to let you know that you have forty-eight hours to do whatever it takes to have the flags restored to their rightful positions. I know that the governor takes the same view of it that I do. I also wanted to let you know that at different times today you may have received various items of bad news from colleagues, friends, and . . . and *family*. While I am sure that these are all coincidental, who knows? If the flags are put back, it is quite possible that another series of random coincidences might occur. In fact, I would probably bet on it. The world is such a quirky place."

Tom paled with fear and flushed with anger at the same time. He could feel both sensations contending within him, and hoped they canceled out. But when he spoke, his voice was calm enough.

"I understand your meaning plainly enough," he said.

"Don't mistake us, though," Parker said. "I am not suggesting that you take forty-eight hours to make up your mind. I am suggesting that you make up your mind as soon as I pull out of your driveway, and use those two days to do whatever needs to be done. Perhaps you will have to convince your stalwart friend to convene a board meeting. Perhaps all you will need to do is walk out to the flag pole and fix things yourself. I don't have a full grasp of how things work . . . at your *Bible* college."

Parker was normally very businesslike and professional in how he conducted himself in such situations, but he did let a note of contempt creep into his voice when he said "Bible college."

"Well, I do thank you for your solicitation and concern," Tom said, standing up. "Whatever else may be said about all this, while the lines may not be drawn for me in pleasant places, they are certainly drawn in *clear* places."

"I always strive for clarity," Parker said.

Tom showed him to the door, said good night with little or no enthusiasm, and when the door was closed, sat down on the bench by the door. He felt as though he had just eaten a couple of the five-pound plates from his weight-lifting gear in the basement. He spent a couple of minutes there searching for the right word. *Effrontery*, that was it.

He collected himself, and headed back to the study. John Melville's name and info would be in his contact list. He glanced at his watch. It was nine thirty. Maybe he could send a quick email, and even talk to him tonight. What time do good lawyers go to bed? Do they even sleep?

He found the info with no difficulty, prayed that John was not the kind of person who changes his email address every two weeks just for fun, and wrote a very brief note. This was just a sounding note, to find out if he was up.

"Dear John," he typed. "I wish I could contact you on a happier occasion. But you may have seen in the news the uproar about the flags that I am involved in. I am contacting you about a related hostage-taking situation that has developed in your city, and if you were available, I wanted to hire you and any minions you might have at your disposal. You still up?"

Send.

Dr. Tom sat at his desk, drumming his fingers, mulling over what he was going to do. He was going to keep fighting, he knew that, but he couldn't let it go so far down the road that Dawn and Frank would lose the girls. But how could he know when he had gotten to that point? Maybe John could help.

His computer chirruped at him. "Still up," the email said. "Can I call you?"

"Call," Tom wrote, and attached his number.

"Give me about ten minutes. Finishing a glass of wine with Kimberly on the deck."

"Okay," Tom wrote back. *Wine. Right. Presbyterians.*

Fifteen minutes later, the phone rang. Tom picked it up with relief. "Hey, John," he said. "Good to hear from you again."

"Hi, Tom. So I think that you contacted me because forces are conspiring against you, but from my perspective, there is a deeper conspiracy at work. I had a desk full of work tomorrow morning that just got canceled because of a plea arrangement that came in at the last minute. I heard about that just about five minutes before your email. So whatever is on your mind, I have a free morning tomorrow to give myself to it. 'The stars fought from their courses against Sisera.'"

Tom laughed a bit. "Well, good. That was one of my worries. I knew you had to be piled up to the rafters with work. But I was prepared to plead my way into your stack anyway."

"No need, apparently. What happened? Besides what I see on the news, I mean? I am all agog."

Tom laughed again, and then told him about the pressures that were being applied—he started with the IRS audits, even though Kramer's stubbornness made them a moot point, at least for the moment. Then he came to the screamer, the threat to Dawn and Frank's girls. "And that is what I want to hire you to go after," he said. "I don't know what can be done, but I want you to do all of that, and about twenty percent more than that."

"Huh," John said. "Numerous options are crowding into my mind . . . but they will be kind of pricey."

"That's the other thing. Pricey doesn't matter. We have it covered."

"Well, I don't hear that every day," John said. "I am going into the office tomorrow first thing, and if you call me at nine, I will have a list of options for you. You can opt for one or all of them. But I do have a warning for you . . ."

"What's that?" Tom said.

"Look," John said. "I am speaking as your attorney here. As your friends, back in Scotland, Kimberly and I appreciated how you and Darla lived your lives in a manner that was completely above reproach, as the apostle put it. But sometimes, and I say this with kindness, you veered a little toward an unnecessary *niceness*. Actually, you were the nicest person in the world. Remember that episode with the auto dealer? And the time at that restaurant? Your mildness in response to provocation can approach iniquitous levels." He paused. "Some of the options I will outline for you tomorrow might make a nice person flinch. You know me. I fight clean, and everything will be above the belt. But it won't be bean bag."

Tom thought of Kirsten and Kelly. "Right," he said. "I would appreciate it if there were no bean bag."

It was John's turn to laugh. "One more thing," he said.

"Shoot," Tom said.

"Have you ever met a man named Trip Akroyd?"

〉〉〉X〈〈〈

Good for his word, John Melville was at his desk the following morning at nine, and had been there for three hours when Dr. Tom called.

"Alright," John said. "Got your pen ready? We do have options."

"Ready," Tom said.

"Let me start by emphasizing the point I made about bean bag. I really believe I can help you, but you have to know how to deal with these people. There is nothing dirty here in what I am going to suggest, nothing unethical, and—more to the point—nothing unbiblical. But some of it might strike the layman as pretty rough stuff."

"Look, John," Tom said. "I trust you. That's why I called you."

"Okay, but remember when the bears ate those delinquents making fun of Elisha? Remember fire coming down out of Heaven and consuming that nameless captain of fifty, along with his fifty? Remember how Miriam danced beside the sea because of what had happened to the horse and rider?"

Tom chuckled. "So you have figured out the modern legal equivalents of Old Testament judgments?"

"No, I wouldn't say that. I just wanted to set a tone for you. Just wanted you to get in the mood."

"Okay, I'm ready."

"The first thing to remember," John said, "is that this kind of thing is always personal, but bureaucrats hide in their institutions, and their first rule is to always keep it looking impersonal. That is their camo. And so, the first thing I want to do is prepare to file a massive lawsuit against the head of Child Protective Services personally—her name is Lois Lantern. And I want to do the same with her assistants."

"Don't you have to sue the agency itself?"

"That depends on what you want them to think. Apart from the merits—and I will tell you in a minute why I think we have a strong case on the merits—I want them to think, right out of the blocks, that *we* think this is personal. We can do this because of what I am alleging, which is that she is acting illegally here on orders from the governor."

"Is that what you meant by the merits?"

"Right," John said. "I have friend who works in the same building that these people do, and he has given me some very reliable information about them being a cat's paw for the governor. You can learn a lot in a government building cafeteria. Sound carries. And from what I know from other sources, I would almost be willing to go for it on that basis. But with this golden source . . . it is not a fishing expedition at all."

"Got it."

"This way, she has to hire an attorney, instead of using the governor's legal counsel."

"Okay with all that. What else have you cooked up?"

"Later today, I am going to be filing about a hundred Freedom of Information requests. I am going to be requesting all the taxpayer-funded email accounts from everybody on the governor's staff."

"Good with that."

They spent the next half hour going over the options, and when they got through John's list, John breathed a sigh of relief. Dr. Tom had hardened significantly since their old days in Scotland together.

They were winding up their discussion when John thought of something. "One other thing," John added, "just so you know. Two weeks ago, I was offered a job by 'Stone' Johnson, Prater's long shot rival. I was on the verge of taking it, but now after talking to you I've decided that would create a conflict of interest for me in taking this case."

"John . . . sorry!" Tom started to exclaim.

"No, no, that's not why I told you. I wanted you to know that I think I can do a whole more for Johnson's campaign taking this case."

9. DEALS WITHIN DEALS

THE FOLLOWING NIGHT WAS THE ANNUAL fund-raising dinner for Choctaw Valley Bible College. Dr. Tom had tried to figure out a time to talk privately with Maria, but because of the fund-raiser, people and appointments were wall-to-wall. The dinner itself was usually a pretty ordinary affair, and Maria could organize it in her sleep. But this one was different. There were record-level registrations, and they had to change the venue twice. In addition, Maria had to arrange for press passes, which had never happened before, and that included reporters from the *New York Times* and the *Washington Post*.

The overt fund-raising part was always pretty low key. An envelope was propped on the centerpiece of every table, and at the end of the evening, the pitch asking everyone to write a check "as the Lord led" was understated, and usually came in at under two minutes. That pitch usually came from Don Carpenter, but tonight Kramer was going to be doing it, which meant that it was probably going to be under a minute.

There was a lot of milling about and handshaking before the meal, and Tom thought that the crowed seemed pretty friendly. At least the people who were willing to talk with him were being friendly. A number of people thanked him for his courage, and there was the record attendance to consider. The atmosphere seemed warm.

So Dr. Tom was thinking that he should get a gracious enough reception when his turn came, but was not at all prepared for what actually happened. He was introduced by Luke Jansen, a popular and gregarious Greek teacher at CVBC, who was the favored emcee at these kinds of events, and as he started to walk toward the lectern, he was startled to see the crowd roar to their feet. Maria was the first one to stand up, and the last one to sit down, which meant that she was applauding for just over five minutes.

These were people who just *hated* being led by trimmers and compromisers, and whose leaders always trimmed and compromised because that is what they thought the people were demanding. They had been let down time and over again by countless leaders who either drifted off into neo-evangelical liberalism like a child's lost carnival balloon, or who blew up in the old-school conservative fashion via sexual scandals. If ever confronted with the possibility of actual battle over the permanent things, they always found a way to avoid it. They could always preach a good sermon about it, denouncing a number of wicked persons elsewhere. But nothing ever seemed to change, perhaps because none of the culprits were ever present.

Dr. Tom was the first fundamentalist leader from their circles in twenty years who had caused a firestorm, and who withstood the first, second, and third assaults that had come at him in response to it. And he had done it without apologizing, backing down, crawling, losing his temper, or imploding. For those reading the papers and watching the news, they knew that this was not because there were no opportunities. Every day that passed without him backing down was yet another astonishment. And so, as a result, the crowd applauded for five minutes straight. There were some tiny little ladies there, now in their eighties, who remembered what they thought were the good old days, and who whooped.

One of the reporters there, the one from the *Washington Post*, described it in his article as a "go-to-hell" ovation. But that wasn't really quite right, because no one in the room would ever talk like that, and if they had talked that way, they would have said that it was a "tired-of-being-told-to-go-to-Hell" ovation. And they would have capitalized Hell, because it was a place. Like Atlanta.

Dr. Tom stood at the lectern during the applause, not quite sure what to do. He caught Maria's eye, smiled, shuffled his notes, smiled an embarrassed smile, and finally just stood there. He looked at Maria again, reflecting on the fact that he had kissed her. *Careful. Not now*, and he reeled it back in. When he thought the crowd was about to sit down, he ventured a "Good evening," but that just set them off again. Tom smiled, thanked God, and just took it.

He had read his speech to Maria and Eve about three times over, and they had been moved by it then. Maria thought it was a really fine speech, but *nothing* had prepared her for how that kite of a speech was going to fly when the winds were gusting like this. The speech was nothing like anything she had ever heard. By the end of it, several of the reporters, one an agnostic and the other spiritual-not-religious, were both wiping their eyes.

Dr. Tom began traditionally enough. "Ladies and gentlemen," he said . . .

$$\rangle\!\rangle\!\rangle\!\rangle\!X\!\langle\!\langle\!\langle$$

When Dr. Tom saw Don Carpenter in the hallway after the event he didn't think anything of it for the first few moments. Don was a fixture at all such events. Of course Don would be there. But then it all came back to him, and the surprise registered on Tom's face. He had just finished shaking hands with a dear lady who had "known his mother, bless her," and he was momentarily free.

Don saw it and walked up to Tom, looking deathly pale, but he extended his hand warmly. "Evening, Tom," he said. "Great speech in there. The best I have ever heard from you."

"Thanks, Don. That means a lot."

"Look, can I ask you something here? Do you have to go?" Don glanced at the small crowd of well-wishers who had gathered immediately after he had begun speaking with Tom. Everyone wanted to shake his hand, and since everyone these days has a camera phone in their pockets, half of them were waiting to take a picture.

"Sure thing, Don. Shoot."

Maria appeared suddenly. "Excuse me, Don. Good news can't wait." She leaned in to whisper in Tom's ear. "We took in somewhere above three hundred thousand dollars. We have *never* done that."

Huh, Don thought. *They seem friendlier than I remember.*

Maria then said, "Sorry. Bye." And she was gone.

"Sorry, Don. Go ahead."

Don bowed his head out of habit, as he was accustomed to do when he was being serious, but then seemed to jerk, and he stood up straight. "Tom, here's the thing. I'll just say it. I haven't been able to sleep since I quit. I still believe everything I told you, which is that I don't have any *professional* confidence we can win this thing long term. But after listening to you tonight, I decided I would rather lose with you than win anywhere else."

Tom was quiet. He didn't trust himself to speak.

"And so," Don continued, "If you haven't advertised my old position, and if you would be willing to forgive me for ditching you at *exactly* the wrong moment, I would like to ask for my old job back."

Tom extended his hand. "Deal," he said. "We haven't done anything. I'll even bet that your chair is still warm."

〉〉〉〈〈〈

Katrina de Paul sat across the desk from her new editor, with whom she was getting along famously. On the desk between them sat a thick manuscript that Katrina had mailed in several months before. Just the week before this meeting, she had received the very good news that the book had been approved in their most recent editorial meeting, and that they were ready to move forward.

So she had arranged to come in for this meeting, and in the course of the meeting discovered that Waterstone Press was *really* interested in moving forward. Like fast.

"The thing that struck our editors," Joanna White said, "was the realization of just how *timely* this book would be." By *timely*, she meant *sensational*. And timely also.

For this manuscript—*Time to Tell*—was a tell-all memoir, and it involved some of Katrina's former lovers, mentioned by name, and in mostly unflattering ways, who would have probably preferred that she not write a book about it. But the problem was that she *had* written a book about it. It was sitting on the desk between Katrina and Joanna.

Katrina had been Fawgee Prater's mistress for a couple of years about ten years before. At the time, after their crack-up, she had thought nothing of it, but as "that odious man" had begun fancying himself as presidential timber, the more she began to think that she needed to get something off her chest. And in public, too.

Another benefit for Katrina, not to be despised, was that she was running a little low on cash, and the advance that was offered by Waterstone was going to be quite generous.

"But the one thing is this," Joanna said. "We would really like to expedite this. Fast-track it. This book would probably sell at any time, but the national campaign is heating up, and we think that the issues you raise in this book are . . . timely." She liked that word.

This editorial meeting had happened three months before the events swirling around the flag poles of Choctaw Valley. And since Waterstone was intent on fast-tracking it—a thing they really could do if they really wanted to—the book was set to release right after Prater was expected to announce what was obvious to everyone already. The manuscript did not allege any illegal activity on his part, but it did allege—and prove—the kind of activity that his base would find hypocritical. Since Prater was seen by the liberal publishing world as the great right-wing threat, it was in their interests to have him blow up right after liftoff. And they wanted the debris field to include everything east of the Mississippi.

Although Prater's was the most "timely" chapter in Katrina's book, his wasn't the only one, of course. There were about ten men named in the book that would be negatively affected. Katrina had been the kind of woman who always seemed to be at important conferences, and who was quite good at networking, and at looking lonesome and beautiful in hotel bars. Some people network by exchanging phone numbers and contact information. She did the same thing, only different. She would be at political conventions, journalism conferences, marketing conferences, and even at philosophy and theology conferences.

The dark horse chapter in *Time to Tell* that no one was really anticipating was the one about Dr. Jake Rollins.

"He was an absurd one," she had written. "He was always looking at his hands."

>>>X<<<

Katrina was not the only one with a book deal. Three months later, and just down the hall, young Abdul was sitting across the desk from an editor. There was nothing to fast-track, because there was no manuscript sitting on the desk. Indeed, there was no manuscript at all.

In this case, Waterstone had sought him out. "We want you to have the fullest opportunity possible to tell your story to a wide audience."

"I appreciate this greatly," Abdul said.

"It is my conviction, and the conviction of our editors," said young Paula Jacobson, "that most Americans don't realize how much hatred out there is still directed against Muslims. We know how things ought to be, and so we just assume that they must be that way."

"I appreciate this greatly," Abdul said.

"But they are not that way at all," Paula said. She had just graduated from Wellesley two years before. She had believed most of what she had been taught in the course of her English major, and all of what she had been taught in her women's studies major.

"We believe," she continued, "that we have a responsibility to show our solidarity with all those who are oppressed by the embedded structures of oppression. Some people think that big publishers are just about the bottom line. But we have a social conscience too. We have responsibilities too."

Abdul nodded encouragingly, and so she continued.

"We see very little difference, for example, in how blacks have been oppressed, and women, and now Muslims. I learned that at Wellesley in my feminist studies—"

"Feminists are whores," Abdul said.

>>>X<<<

Norman Greenbaum—"no, not that one," he was always saying—glared at the men around the table. As one of the ACLU's foremost lawyers, he'd had numerous meetings about the flag issue. The ACLU was always involved in flag cases. How could there be a flag case with them *not* involved in it?

The problem was that they needed to decide how they were going to do it. Virtually all of them agreed that they needed to not be on the side of Dr. Tom, but after that, they quickly went to stalemate. Half of them thought that filing a brief on the side of what they thought the governor was probably going to do would make them look even-handed. "Prater is a Republican, and our agreement would throw everybody."

But the others, Greenbaum included, thought that doing anything would just expose a massive inconsistency in their position. "I don't look forward to having to explain to everybody why it is not okay to pull the flag down three feet lower than another flag, but why it would be okay to haul it all the way down the pole in order to pee on it. My instincts are with you all, gentlemen. I would just like to have something rational to say when people ask us about it. For they will ask us about it."

And so they kept having meetings, and they kept not coming to a decision, and reporters would periodically call and ask them if they had any statement yet, and they never did. Another of their number, a bright young one from Harvard, said, "You know that not doing something is going to become the story at some point. You do know that, right?"

Everybody said right. But nobody knew what to do, and they were divided on what they should be sure not to do.

10. A TALE OF TWO HONOR GUARDS

DR. TOM HAD BEEN USING UP EVERY NOOK AND cranny of his free moments thinking about it. He realized fully what he wanted to do, but the situation with the flag fiasco now seemed so dire that he was not sure he should have dragged Maria into it. *Should have thought of that before you kissed her, champ.* Besides, she was his administrative assistant, and she was already in the thick of it. And on top of that, it was in Narnia that you got to kiss the girl after slaying the dragon. In this world, you kissed her first. That's what the stories plainly said.

Of course Maria was still alternating between fits of exultant expectation and utter despondency, depending on her hermeneutic when she reread Tom's email, which she had done several hundred times, and that hermeneutic in its turn depended on her mood and what mood she had *previously* been in.

The first morning Tom was back from New York, his schedule was crammed full, couldn't be helped, but there was an unexpected no-show for the eleven o'clock, and so Tom had a half hour in his schedule that wasn't full up with something urgent and tyrannical. He suddenly appeared by her desk, and asked if he could talk with her for a minute.

She nodded, and came into his office behind him, swallowing nervously. *He's going to apologize for kissing me.* They both sat down in the wing backs.

"I . . . I had no business kissing you like that in New York, and I would like to apologize for it."

"I . . . I didn't mind." *Gross understatement, Maria.* Just as she was prepared for him to apologize, she was also prepared with a question she had gone over in her mind a hundred times or so. "If you don't mind me asking, why do you think you should apologize?" *You dear, sweet fathead.*

Tom was fooling around with something in his hands. "Well . . . I really don't believe I should have done anything like that unless I had a ring with me to give to you."

"I see. I understand." Maria nodded, not understanding.

"And the ring is a family heirloom, and it was back here at my house. Here it is." Tom extended the ring to her.

"Oh!" Maria suddenly understood. They both were suddenly on their feet, and a second later they were in each other's arms. Tom kissed her again, stepped back, and helped her put the ring on her finger. He hesitated at the last minute. "I don't want to presume, or be too pushy . . . do you really want it?"

Maria nodded, and then nodded again, wiping her eyes.

About fifteen minutes later, Maria came out to the reception area, and sat down at her desk, trying very hard not to glow. In this she was singularly unsuccessful, and Eve, sitting at her desk across the way, just took a few moments before she asked, "What happened in there?" Maria held up her left hand, fingers splayed, palm in.

Eve hopped up and ran over. "Aaaaaaa!" She stopped and clapped her hands. "Yay! Mrs. Dr. Tom!"

>>>X<<<

A friend of Trevor's from the gym downtown was a cop with the reserves, and, of course, if it comes to that, why shouldn't he have been? Kent, for that was his name, called Trevor the same evening that Dr. Tom and Maria got engaged.

"Listen, Trev, the only reason I am calling is that I know how *bogus* this whole thing is."

"Well, thanks," Trevor said. "But *what* is bogus?"

"The chief says that the governor, full of impatience, has the wrath of man sloshing around inside him."

And this was indeed the case. Gov. Prater, filled with
the kind of aggrieved righteousness that you usually see in
a cat that has just been hosed down by a ten-year-old boy,
had decided that it was time to act. Even though he had told
Parkson to give the hold-out forty-eight hours for "decisions,"
the more the minutes staggered through his mental turnstile,
the more he didn't want to wait that long.

And so it was that he decided to send a liberation party
to "rescue" the American flag from the place of dishonor
that Choctaw Valley Bible College had given to it, and a
press entourage was to follow in their wake, surging back
and forth.

Kent continued, "They called up the reserves to watch the
fort, while all the regular forces of our commonwealth, including a bunch of guys in riot gear, are on display. I swear,
he would have gotten some warships involved if we weren't
so far inland. It is going to be some kind of show, Trev. Not
that I think you can do anything, but I thought somebody
over there should know. And I wanted you to know how embarrassed I am to be associated with law enforcement. I am
thinking of opening up a yarn shop instead. My mom used
to knit."

"Thanks, Kent. Thanks for the call. Gotta go. Gotta think."

Trevor did not know what he could possibly do, but he did
know that he was going to do *something*. If it came down to it,
if he hadn't thought of something by morning, he would just

hop in the car and drive until he wound up doing something. But he needed to think of something that would leave the solons of his fair state just sitting there, scratching their beards.

He looked at his watch. *Eve!* He was meeting Eve for a late dinner in fifteen minutes. So many things to think about. He needed to multitask, and he wasn't any good at it. He needed a helpmeet.

〉〉〉X〈〈〈

The meal had gone smoothly and well. Trevor held up his end of the conversation, but he wasn't going at his ordinary torrential pace. Eve could tell something was on his mind.

"Is something on your mind?" she asked sweetly.

"Well, yes, several things," he said. "I am trying to sort out what order they should go in, and neither order makes sense. Each one sort of spoils the other."

"Well, pick the one that you think would be most fun to start with. Life is uncertain. Eat dessert first."

"All right, then." Trevor said. "The lady has spoken. Here, let's go."

They walked out the front of the restaurant, and turned left to walk back up to campus, which was only about a block away. They walked in silence, with Eve wondering when Trevor would get to it, and Trevor waiting until they got to the place that lined up with what he had planned.

When they had rounded the first big corner in the path, Trevor suddenly pointed up ahead. "Look! Look at that elm."

Eve could tell he was up to something. "Well, I do see it."

"A wonderful place for a first kiss, wouldn't you think?"

Eve smiled, and said nothing.

After a minute or so, Trevor announced again, "Glory! The lady is still walking in that direction. Despite being warned."

"Well, I don't see why the lady—as you so romantically call her—wouldn't want to be kissed there as much as the gentleman seems to want to."

Trevor cleared his throat. "For starters, that wouldn't be possible, I don't think. And in the second place, I believe it is customary for the lady to face the gentleman. Like this."

She smiled up at him. "And then?"

"And then this." A moment later he stepped back. "Well, I can die now."

"Please don't. Were you going to kiss me again?"

"I think I had better not. 'Do not awaken love before the time.' Canticles 2:7."

"Too late for that, sport. But if you aren't going to kiss me ag— . . . " She stopped when he kissed her again.

A minute later, they stepped apart. Eve reached out and rubbed the back of his neck. "Well, having established our *entente cordiale*, perhaps we had better be going."

"French, eh? Kind of swanky. I am starting to think I am not good enough for you."

"Don't forget that I am a Canadian. From Alberta. The French thing doesn't really signify the same thing up there."

"Well, that's a relief." Trevor held out his hand. As soon as he took it, he clutched his forehead with his other hand. "I knew I was forgetting something! Eve, will you marry me?"

She said, "Let me think about it, yes."

》》X《《

So Trevor and Eve made the rounds, telling all their friends about their engagement, and, for those who hadn't heard about it, about the engagement of Dr. Tom and Maria.

"In fact," Trevor said suspiciously, "this is starting to look like the end of a Gilbert and Sullivan. But I don't know how the classic comedic ending can truly satisfy with this other . . . trouble hanging over us."

"Tell me about this other thing," Eve said. "Maybe mother can help."

And so Trevor laid the whole thing out for her. The governor and his minions are going to show up on campus in the morning to rescue the flag. "And we can't take it down before they get here, because that would be doing what they wanted—it would look like capitulation, whether or not it was. And I could just go tell Dr. Tom, but I don't know what he could do. I have a gut feeling that this will have to be accomplished by his guerrilla forces."

Eve sat back in her chair. "That is a stumper."

"You betcher," Trevor said.

And Eve sat forward again, having leaned back for approximately five seconds. "So here is what we can do."

Trevor saw the look on her face, and his doubts vanished. Whatever she was going to suggest was going to be a pippin, just like *she* was. "'She openeth her mouth with wisdom.' Proverbs 31:26," he said. "What is it?"

"Well, let me tell you a story," she said. "The moral and possible applications should be plain as I approach the end of my tale."

"Go right ahead," he said, staring at how the line of her jaw came up to her ear.

"One time, when I was a little girl," she said, "and I took a dimmer view of boys than I do now—*now* I think they can be sweet—my two friends and I were involved in a pine cone war with my two brothers and one of their friends from the neighborhood. They had their tree fort, and we had a walk-in playhouse in the back corner of the yard, one my dad built for me. The battle raged through the morning, with many pine cones thrown. Because we were enemy combatants, we took lunch in different houses. Billy's mom fed them across the alley, and our mom fed us girls at our house. With me still?"

"Forever," Trevor said.

"Well, we were finishing our sandwiches, and looked out the back window, and what did we see? We saw three boys in *our* playhouse, grimacing at us, making boy faces. Under the sacred lunch truce, they had come back early, and had captured our fortress—note the feminine ending—and were doing little boy victory dances inside of it. It was not a happy time around our lunch table, let me assure you."

In spite of her jaw, and ear, and neck, Trevor was now in story grip. "What happened?"

"My mother—whom you will love, by the way—took us into the garage, and laid out a plan for us. It was elegant, brilliant, and I have never stopped admiring her since."

Trevor was looking impatient, so Eve hastened on.

"She had us hop in the car, and drove us around the block and down the alley. She stopped, right by the base of the boy's tree fort. We hopped out, and were up the rope ladder in about ten seconds, and pulled the ladder up after us. The boys... well, I can't rightly say how upset they were. They were hopping around the base of the tree, throwing pine cones, but we were out of range. We had just had lunch, and had all used the bathroom before the raid, so we were good for at least three hours up there. So we just looked over the railing, and spoke to them sweetly."

"So," Trevor said, "I am having the glimmering of an idea, but how would you apply this?"

"So the governor wants to take a flag down here? Let us, in the same time frame, put up a flag at his place."

Trevor sat for a moment, amazed. "A jewel among women," he said. "And I get to marry her! The idea is yours, oh, mighty Deborah. May I organize it?"

"Please do."

Trevor already had his phone out, and was typing in names and instructions. Tomorrow would be glorious.

>>>X<<<

And so it was, at ten the following morning, by order of the governor, a SWAT team (ordered by the mayor of the city, a crony of the governor), backed by the National Guard (ordered by the governor himself), attended by multiple state troopers, arrived the next morning in full regalia and rescued the flag. The word *regalia* is broad, and can encompass many things. There were men in full camo gear. There were men in riot gear. There were men with walkie-talkies and badges around their necks. There were two men in ghillie suits, which no one took responsibility for, and of course there were many serious members of law enforcement with big block letters on the backs of their windbreakers. Fawgee Prater had never seen the mobilization of law enforcement at the end of *The Blues Brothers*, but he would have approved of it if he had.

The convoy drove up the drive of the college, and once the advance team had secured the perimeter of the little grassy mound that had the flag poles on it, the governor's limo drove up, followed by many, many camera teams. The armed forces assembled there had fanned out across the lawn, looking prepared for anything short of a full-scale invasion. In the background of some of the news shots, an occasional student could be seen walking to class.

As someone running for president, the governor knew that a good photo op was gold. He waited until the cameras were set up and running, and strode purposefully toward the shorter flag pole where the stars and stripes were hanging dejectedly—there was no breeze—and untied the knot, and personally hauled down the flag, cameras clattering and whirring as he did so. When he was done, he walked down the drive toward the gates, past which Mrs. McCorkadale had matched wits with Trevor and lost. Just outside the gate, he had arranged for a full honor guard to meet him. They were from the ROTC unit over at Behemoth State—the pee-on-the-flag university.

The governor got most of the way to the gate, and then stopped so some of the slower reporters and photographers could catch up. And then, head bowed in respect, he walked out and handed the flag to the guard. Then he stepped back about five paces, and watched solemnly as the flag was folded, smartly, diagonally, and according the correct protocols. When they were done, he turned and faced the reporters, spoke a few words that were suitably brief and respectful, including the theme that this Bible college didn't deserve to fly the flag at all, and then concluded with, "Well, let us leave this place."

The photos were statesmanlike.

>>>X(((

Trevor thought that he could coordinate about 120 students, enough for a great photo. But the only ones who knew
what the plan was going to be were part of Trevor and Eve's
close associates. "They will find out what we are doing when
we have done it. We can't afford any leaks."

The governor's mansion was stately, beautiful . . . and the
front entry was open to the public. As you walked up the
main drive, you came to a Y in the road, the right side going
down to where the lines formed for tours, and the left side
working up to the main entrance. In front of the main entrance, about fifty feet straight out in front of the doors, was a
small grassy mound, about the same size and shape of the one
at Choctaw Valley. There were only two flagpoles there, one
for the American flag and the other for the state flag.

The flash mob was quietly assembling outside the wrought-
iron gate, which looked forbidding, but was still open. Trevor
told them to keep walking back and forth, at least fifty yards
out, so that no one would think a mob was assembling and
call security.

Trevor had a brown bag under his arm, containing the
Christian flag that he had gotten from the chapel. When he
thought he had enough students for the photo, and the time
appointed had passed by about five minutes, Trevor put his
little fingers in his mouth and whistled. This was the signal to

assemble together, which happened silently, in two minutes, and then *go*. All together the students began walking, steadily, silently. "Don't run," Trevor had said. "Nobody seems to be looking, but we don't want to spook them if they do."

Three volunteer photographers veered off to the left so that they could get a good picture of the spectacle. One had a regular camera, and the other two had iPhones. "As soon as you two get your photos, email them to your entire contact list—in case our cameras are confiscated."

The massed students made it to the flag pole with no trouble, and gathered behind it, turning to face the cameras. Trevor untied the rope, and briskly hauled the American flag down. He handed it to a couple of the students who had been Boy Scouts, and who knew how to fold the flag, and hooked up the Christian flag, and up it went.

One of the boys who had folded the flag shook his head and said, "I don't get it. They can just put their flag back up again."

"Ah," Trevor said. "Digital images and the Internet are more difficult to replace than that. I have Duane waiting by his laptop—as soon as he has a photo of the governor at our flag pole, which he should be able to get off any news site any minute now, and as soon as he has the photo that Darlene over there has just sent him, he will be able to create a classic meme, one for the ages."

And so it was. An iconic photo emerged by the end of that day, with the photo on top showing the governor, with his assembled firepower, taking down the American flag at a sleepy little Bible college. The photo at the bottom showed a collection of cheerful college students standing in front of the governor's mansion, with the Christian flag atop the flagpole there, unfolded in a providential breeze.

In block white letters, across both photographs, the caption ran, "So the governor wants to play capture the flag, does he?"

II. THE FINAL FLAG

THE SUN HAD BARELY GOTTEN ONE ELBOW ON THE edge of the world that constituted the top of his garden wall. It was the morning after the capture-the-flag meme exploded on the Internet, and the governor was furious. He had already been up for several hours, scrolling through all the different forms of laughter at his expense that his browser could serve up. And he was taking it with an ill grace.

When enough of a staff assembled to constitute a quorum for getting yelled at, in the presence of his secretary Susan, Parker Parkson, and two interns, he dumped out two buckets of cuss words onto the carpet, and then spent a good ten minutes kicking them around the room with his cowboy boots.

One of the interns had been around the offices for a while, and so he was able to take it all in stride. Besides, he had a grandfather who talked like that. But for the other intern, whose name was Wendell, this was his first true introduction to Fawgee Prater's approach to governance, and it was not at *all* what he was expecting. Public spiritedness, it seemed to him, ought to take other forms.

As the ancient Romans noted, anger is a brief madness. In anger, carelessness is born. Trip Akroyd had made that very observation in his discussion with Dr. Tom.

Parker Parkson was just glad the governor seemed to be getting it out of his system. In just few hours, he was going to be driven up to a place in the hills that had a great deal of symbolic photo op value to the voters, in kind of a Groundhog Day fashion, but which had little value otherwise. Somewhere, back in the early twentieth century, some candidate or other had managed to make a visit to Toad Flats mandatory for everyone else who was to come thereafter. Davy Crockett had come through that same place once, and had shot a bear out of a tree, or so they said. Making the trek had become almost synonymous with democracy. There were about seventeen votes total at stake, but for mysterious reasons it had become a *necessary* photo op that every other voter in the state expected. Nobody noticed when it happened, but if it ever *didn't* happen, no one who wanted to get elected to anything was prepared to answer for the consequences.

So, Parker thought, better here than there. Better to us than to dear Miss Sally, standing there horrified behind the ancient counter that had been made out of the tree that Davy Crockett shot the bear out of.

Everybody knew that this was a campaign stop—but it was not *official* because the governor had not yet declared. And because it was *unofficially* configured, this meant that the state would pay for it. So Parker was happy. He was also happy because the governor seemed to come off the full boil after he had expressed his sentiments fully.

But unknown to Parker, the governor was still on a high simmer. He was full of dark thoughts and recriminations. He had vented fully, and was nevertheless still full. Things were not going well for him, he felt. Something was stuck, and this translated into a surging desire to ream *everybody* on his staff that had anything whatever to do with the flag debacle. The four recipients of his first round of ministrations were clearly not sufficient. This desire for self-expression continued to rise within him all morning, like magma under Yellowstone, until he came to the conviction that life, as it was currently shambling along, was entirely unbearable.

Wendell was appointed to be his driver, and he took the assignment like a man. Perhaps the drive would enable him to get to know the governor on a human level, even though he thought that the point could be argued that he had already seen more than enough of that.

The drive up was silent. The governor spent his time staring morbidly out the window. After a hour or thereabouts,
they rounded the final curve and descended into the moun-
tain valley where the denizens of Toad Flats lived the high
life. It was a quaint little bend-in-the-road town that had
one road-stop cafe and gift shop, and a gas station across the
street. Prater had been up there a number of times before in
order to glad-hand the customers, so he knew the ropes. He
went through the motions like a pro, just as he had done in
the years previously. He then said a few words to the folks
who had gathered at the cafe, answered a few questions,
mostly about the Second Amendment, bought a couple jars
of jelly, shook a few more hands, and headed back to the car.

Wendell had really been rattled by that morning's out-
burst. He had not recognized half of the words used, but
was certainly able to catch the general drift. He had already
been somewhat afraid of the governor, then he had gotten the
treatment, the drive up had been ominous, and now here he
was in the same car with him for the hour back.

They both climbed in the car, and the governor, done
with meditative fuming, was ready to write, and so he started
rummaging in his pack, looking for his laptop. After just a
few moments, it became apparent that he had left it behind,
back in town, and as they wound down the road away from
Toad Flats, the governor did his cussing act again, each word
hitting young Wendell on his right cheek and ear like a cold

mackerel, thrown from the back seat. None of it was a pleasing sensation.

"You could use my computer," Wendell finally ventured.

His full name was Wendell P. Hodges III. *Nobody* was more interested in doing the right thing than he was, and he was the kind of young man who defined the "right thing" by the book, whatever "the book" happened to be. He was a policies and procedures man, and the lawlessness apparent in the governor's demeanor, conversation, instructions, and so forth, had been a pebble in Wendell's shoe from the second day of his arrival on staff. He had gotten the internship because of the pull his grandmother had, and her convictions and demeanor were of a similar nature to his. If she had been a piano, she would have been a nineteenth-century upright.

But at the same time, this very same grandmother was as fully convinced as a person can be convinced, for reasons known only to providence, that Gov. Fawgee Prater was the only possible hope for the Republic. She and the governor's mother had been in Kappa Kappa Gamma together, and that went for a lot. To allege corruption in Prater's inner circle would have been, for her, an attempt to square the circle. She had no category for it. She was unlike the governor as it would be possible for a human being to be, and yet at the same time, she thought the governor was *wonderful*. It only goes to show what living two hundred miles away can do for someone.

Wendell Hodges was acutely aware of all this. He could not quit his position as intern without explaining it to his grandmother, which he did not have the capacity to do, and he could not remain there without becoming the kind of sleazebucket that everyone else surrounding the governor appeared to be. In short, Wendell P. Hodges III was in quite a jam.

Even though he was in a big-picture jam, he had still managed to fix the current missing-computer problem the governor had. The governor grunted in a mollified sort of way and pulled out Wendell's laptop, fired it up, logged into his email account, and began to type furiously. It was an epic email, containing all the words he had just been using, and then some. He was making himself feel better by the minute.

As they were pulling into the back drive going up to the governor's mansion, he was just finishing. When he clicked *send*, the car was pulling to a stop. Parker Parkson was standing by the back door talking to the press secretary, and saw that it was the governor. He had some news to share, apparently, and started walking toward the car. The governor saw Parkson coming, snapped the lid of the computer shut out of habit, got out of the car, and gestured to Wendell to drive off. The gesture did not quite mean that the driving off should be done from the nearest pier, but it came close. Wendell drove slowly home, chewing on his lip.

After his glum dinner of ramen and chopped up hot dogs, Wendell flipped open his computer to check his email, and absentmindedly read halfway through the first one. Then he stopped, as though a high voltage shot of electricity had gone through him, which it very nearly had. The contents of what he was reading dawned on him. *This wasn't his email account. The governor had forgotten to log out.* And this email was from the head of Child Protective Services, a woman named Lois Lantern, telling the governor that everything was going most satisfactorily. Dr. Tom's sister Dawn and her husband Frank were absolutely on the hook, and everything was looking quite good. The governor had nothing to worry about. Bible-college boy was sure to buckle now.

This email from Lois was intended as a reassuring response to the governor's email that he had typed in the car, and his letter had been pretty ripe, and just *full* of information. Wendell looked up at the number of messages in the back and forth thread, prior to this day's exchanges. There were seventeen of them. Would it be evil to read them? He already had read enough to be damning. What was the right thing to do? What were the *procedures*? He couldn't not know what he already knew, could he? How do you unknow something?

He knew that he was in possession of hot property. He also knew that he could not do anything with it, and he also knew he could not *not* do anything with it. He had played basketball in high school, and he was the kind of guy who, whenever he was nervous about taking a three-pointer, would always pass it off. *That* was the ticket. He moved the whole thing to a thumb drive, and then sat there at his kitchen table, having a soul crisis. Who could he pass it to?

Wendell Hodges had known Trevor Smith from flight school a couple of years before. He also had figured out, from all the names that had been thrown around in the governor's various outbursts, that Trevor was serving Dr. Collins of Choctaw Valley in *some* kind of capacity. And some reporter had emailed the governor's office a photo he had taken of Trevor, standing on the base of the Whitefield statue, that day when he was busy being the victorious general at the Battle of Choctaw Valley. It was pinned to the bulletin board in the war room. Wendell had recognized Trevor right off.

Wendell's feelings toward Trevor had always been mixed. He admired his abilities and cheerfulness, and yet he was put off somewhat by Trevor's moral center apparently having nothing whatever to do with any procedure manuals. And they had been rivals of a sort in flight school, each vying for the coveted student pilot award that the school offered to one member of each graduating class. Wendell had actually won that award, and Trevor had just laughed like it was the greatest thing in the world, and had shaken Wendell's hand as though Wendell had just saved Trevor's life. He was a weird guy.

Finally, after about two hours of chewing on it, he got a small padded envelope from his desk organizer, looked up the address of Choctaw Valley, and sent it to the main office, attn. Trevor Smith. Trevor was enough of an antinomian not to have any angst about this kind of thing at all. But he wasn't the same kind of antinomian that the governor was, that was for sure.

〉〉〉〈〈〈

Maria looked at the padded envelope quizzically, and texted Trevor, saying there was a package for him at the office. He came by and picked it up later that morning, and Maria promptly forgot all about it. She even forgot to mention it to Tom. They had other things to talk about—even though they were both were in the midst of the biggest crisis that Choctaw Valley had ever had, they were both having trouble keeping their heads in the game. They had both underestimated—Tom more than Maria—what a declaration of love's intent was going to do to all their waking thoughts. If it hadn't been for Tom's nieces, he wouldn't have been in the game at all.

Trevor promptly read through all the emails in the thread sent to him, danced around his apartment briefly, and then spent a couple hours setting up a spreadsheet with all the damning bits of information cataloged according to the nature of the offense. He thought, *perhaps* correctly, that Dr. Tom might have a scruple or two about using this kind of information, and so he wisely decided to let this effort be his

little secret. He then went to a coffee shop to set up an anonymous Twitter account, and started releasing excerpts from
the thumb drive, 140 characters or less at a time, always including the hash tag *#WhistleBlowersGottaTweet*.

The first went right to the solar plexus.

> #CPS Lois Lantern targets Dr. Tom's relatives on
> Prater's orders #WhistleBlowersGottaTweet

The second was sent the following afternoon.

> Gov. Prater takes your kids away if you are related to
> Dr. Tom #FamilyValues #WhistleBlowersGottaTweet

Now Trevor felt entirely comfortable with this, because if
he got caught, he had the goods. He could back up everything
he was writing. Speaking of backing up, he wrapped the thumb
drive in cellophane and buried it in the potting soil of the flow-
er his sister had sent to him. His sister was going to *love* Eve.

With some effort, he yanked his mind back to the task at
hand. Because he was withholding most of the goods, not
releasing everything all at once, the bad guys were not in a
position to know just how many of the goods he had. Or who
"he" was, for that matter.

In a burst of poetic inspiration, Trevor had decided to
release each day's revelatory Tweet at exactly 2:20 in the

afternoon. 220 Magnolia was the governor's private address, a datum that was picked up on by one astute reporter after about five days.

But it only took two days for it to assume the proportions of a big stink. After a day or so, the press corps started asking questions about it. Reporters begin to look forward to them. In the press conference where it first came up, the governor bloviated in a way that was probably his finest performance ever. But back in the offices, he went into a high panic, accompanied by his usual blue vocabulary. But this time the words were flying over all their heads in a missing man formation.

This *had* to be a whistleblower on his staff, and it had to be someone who was in deep—the things that were being released in the tweets—the names, the comments, the links— were all uber-secrets. The one person in the entire operation upon whom suspicion did *not* fall was Wendell. *He* had access to nothing. After a few days of nobody looking at him funny at all, in any way, Wendell started to cautiously peer out of his emotional cave. Maybe this would all end in a way that would enable him to look his grandma in the eye, which in fact, is actually what happened.

After a week, because of a stray comment made at a press conference by one of his rivals to the Republican nomination, and the only one from the same state, the governor assumed— naturally enough—that *this* was the opposing campaign that was behind the stream of tweets. He had Parker scouring the backgrounds of everybody in his campaign who had ever done anything with anyone in "Stone" Johnson's campaign. This was pretty time-consuming because Republican politics in the state was pretty ingrown. Pretty much everybody had done something with somebody.

"Stone" Johnson's was a campaign with some integrity— at least, that's what people with some integrity themselves said—and that was in turn the factor that made Prater assume that Johnson was the culprit. The others were rivals— dogs fighting over a piece of meat. Johnson was an *adversary*.

The subject matter of the initial tweets was all about Dawn and Frank, and their two hostage kids, which didn't have anything directly to do with the coming campaign, but as the governor's anger grew in its white-hottedness, it was all directed at his political rival. The Christian flag at Choctaw Valley was scarcely mentioned at staff meetings anymore. Reporters stopped asking about it.

Trevor continued tweeting with metronome-like regularity. At the beginning of the third week, Trevor decided to move on to the drip-drip-drip tweet hints concerning the IRS audits of the board members who voted for Tom, one a day.

When, in the determination of Parker Parkson, the controversy had hit critical mass, the governor called a press conference. He promised to stay at the podium until all these baseless charges have been answered, one by one, if necessary.

But unbeknownst to the governor, all the reporters were showing up well-armed beforehand, each with a different missile. John Melville had let the guy from the *Tribune* know that he had, that very morning, filed a massive lawsuit against Lois Lantern and three of her assistants in alphabetical order. The reporter from *The New York Times* had received, two nights before, an advance reader's copy of *Time to Tell*, with certain key passages marked with Post-It Notes. Another reporter, with a local television station, had received a call from Lois at CPS letting him know that they were dropping the case against Frank and Dawn. And three other reporters had each received an anonymous email from whistleblowersgottatweet@yahoo.com, each of them different, with an attachment showing high collusion between the governor and various functionaries at the IRS.

The governor had a *very* long afternoon, and when it was over, there was hardly any chum left in the water at all. The sharks had eaten all of his presidential aspirations—and he was probably going to jail. The Republic was safe for the present, and John Melville resigned his position as partner in his law firm in order to become the chief advisor to "Stone" Johnson. It was a shrewd move.

>>>X<<<

In the quiet aftermath of all the controversy, Tom and Maria liked to take a walk in the late afternoon, every afternoon, once all the classes were out for the day. They liked to walk down to the wooden bridge where all the seniors would go to get engaged, down by the arboretum.

As they were walking on this particular evening, Maria decided to just go ahead. "Can I tell you about something?"

"Sure."

"A year ago, more than that, actually, probably two years, before all this happened, I used to go home at night and think about you for hours. I even cried a few times. Did you know that?"

Tom cleared his throat sympathetically. He stammered, "I . . . I had no idea . . ."

"Did . . . did you ever think that way about me?"

Tom shook his head. "No . . . well, to be perfectly honest, I wouldn't ever let myself think about you. Not for any length of time at all."

Maria looked startled, and tried not to be a tad hurt. "Why ever not?"

"Because after about thirty seconds it would always get wildly inappropriate."

Maria laughed, and even in the twilight, Tom could see that she was blushing. "Well, I suppose I should take that as a compliment."

"Oh, absolutely. I'll tell you more about it later. After we're married. Later. Some other time. *Later.*"

"You're serious!"

"Oh, yes. Every time it happened, I'd go out in the back yard and dig a hole. The next day I'd go to the garden store and get a bush or a tree to plant there. Helped keep my mind where an unmarried Bible college president's mind ought to have been. On yard upkeep. And on things above."

"You'd go out and plant one tree . . . ?"

"It's kind of a wilderness area now."

Maria laughed, and patted his chest three times. "You poor baby. When the right time comes, which by my reckoning is just fourteen days from now, I have just what it takes to fix you right up."

"Well, I am sure," Tom remarked, looking at the late afternoon sky, "that I have no idea what you are talking about."

"It's an old trick my mother told me about. She swore by it. Said it worked every time."

This time it was his turn to blush. They both laughed at the same time, hooked their little fingers together—because they both knew in a moment like that any more contact wouldn't have been safe—and walked out onto the wooden bridge to play Poohsticks with pine cones in the water.

>>>X<<<

After their honeymoon, Tom Collins consulted with his board, and then gave final orders that the American flag not be replaced, and that the Christian flag continue to fly on the central and tallest pole. A few months later, he was asked at a news conference by a reporter from the *Weekly Bee* why the American flag was no longer flying.

"Somebody stole it," Tom said.

42075676R00116